Joy
in the
Morning

Joy
in the
Morning

Sandra Lumbrezer

TATE PUBLISHING
AND ENTERPRISES, LLC

Published by Tate Publishing & Enterprises, LLC
127 E. Trade Center Terrace | Mustang, Oklahoma 73064 USA
1.888.361.9473 | www.tatepublishing.com

Tate Publishing is committed to excellence in the publishing industry. The company reflects the philosophy established by the founders, based on Psalm 68:11,
"The Lord gave the word and great was the company of those who published it."

Book design copyright © 2016 by Tate Publishing, LLC. All rights reserved.
Cover design by Samson Lim
Interior design by Gram Telen

Published in the United States of America

ISBN: 978-1-68319-309-8
Fiction / Christian / General
16.04.19

Contents

1	Porter's Bend	9
2	The Beautiful Land	12
3	George and Anna	16
4	Church	20
5	Fanny's First Year of School	27
6	Girl in the Mirror	35
7	Love Works a Miracle	39
8	A Good Neighbor	46
9	A Father's Love	55
10	When the Future Plans Itself	59
11	Kingston!	64
12	Wishing and Hoping	71
13	A Day to Remember	81
14	The Ups and Downs of Friendship	86
15	Fulfillment of Duty	89
16	Decisions	94
17	Chicago	99
18	Dressing for the Part	111

19 Consequences 114

20 A Problem or a Blessing? 120

21 A Place for Fanny 123

22 Going Back Home 131

23 Brothers 140

24 Hanging by a Thread 145

25 Timothy 150

26 Chance Encounter 153

27 Losing a Friend and Gaining Another 158

28 Love Finds Fanny 163

29 Disappointment 169

30 The Proposal 173

31 Elizabeth 175

32 The Cold Hard Truth 180

33 Jane Anne 188

34 Letter from Jimmy 190

35 The Healing Touch 193

36 New Events 200

37 All Things for Our Good 206

38 Starting to Heal 208

39 A Second Blessing 211

40 Jane Comes Home..216

41 The Mission Field..220

42 Joy and Trials..229

43 Revelation..233

44 A Time to Leave...235

45 All Things for Our Good....................................239

46 Starting to Heal...245

47 A Second Blessing...250

48 Going Home...254

49 The Mission Field..258

50 Joy and Trials..265

51 Toby...271

52 Turning Point..275

53 Complications..287

54 Waiting for an Answer.......................................290

55 Best of Plans..296

56 Overheard..300

57 Audie Comes Home...303

58 Tragedy..306

59 Joy in the Morning..312

1

Porter's Bend

It began with a sod shanty built into the side of a hill. The shanty was put together in 1890 by Joshua Taylor. At that time, he was a single young man who bought the thirty acres or so of land that was nestled at the foot of Bear Mountain, where the Holden River runs through. Taylor had hopes of farming out a portion of the land with cotton or tobacco. These were sure fire cash crops, and once he saved enough, he planned on building a regular house. His hope was to meet a good Christian woman to be his wife and bear his children. Brought up by devoted Baptists from central Kentucky, he longed for a family he could call his own. His mother and father had been wonderful parents, personifying how satisfying having a marriage and family could be. Watching them had inspired Josh Taylor to carve out a similar life of his own.

So he set out for Tennessee at the age of seventeen with only a few dollars in his pocket. His mother and father wished him well with his search for a new life. So he set out with a head and heart full of desires and dreams for a bright future.

The town across the Holden River was called Kingston, and there Josh found work in a paper factory unloading the lumber used to make the paper. He carefully counted and saved each dollar he earned each week. He spent his nights sleeping in the office area of the factory and washing up in the horse trough in the early morning before others in town were awake. When he had accumulated a good sum of money, he went to the land office in Kingston and bought the land where he hoped to live and work the rest of his life. He had built the sod shanty as a short-term home but had no idea just how short that time would be.

A month after Josh Taylor had acquired his land, he developed a respiratory ailment that quickly spiraled into pneumonia. Too weak to go into town for medical care, he suffered through his sickness until he drew his last breath and died.

A neighbor with land adjacent to Taylor's chased a pheasant near the sod shanty. "Hallooo!" he called as he opened the canvas that served as a door covering. As the outside light cast its glow inside the sod house, the hunter saw a figure lying on a pile of meadow grass unmoving. Investigating further, he found young Josh Taylor dead. He felt some sorrow for the dead man and, as a Christian man, felt it was his duty to bury him and say a short prayer for God to take his soul to be with Him. He went into

Kingston directly and informed the authorities that he had found and buried the man who lived at the foot of Bear Mountain.

No one in Kingston or thereabouts knew if Taylor had a next of kin, so the land went back to the state of Tennessee. Over the course of a few years, the acres were parceled out to a dozen or so folks, creating something of a small community. The homes were mostly common structures built by folks who wanted to get away from the noise and dirt of the city. Kingston was growing from what had once been a small town. Industry was on a speedy incline bringing people from all over the country looking for work. The sights and smells of an industrial center was soon becoming the heart of Kingston.

Just beyond the Holden River, at the foot of Bear Mountain, the scenery was still unspoiled. It remained as pure and pristine as it had been a hundred years before. This was a beautiful place for those that chose an escape from the smelly factories and the fast pace of city life. It became known as Porter's Bend because Abraham Porter built the first real house there near a bend in the Holden River. Even in this last regard, Joshua Taylor was denied any remembrance of his existence there.

2

The Beautiful Land

What had drawn Joshua Taylor to this place now known as Porter's Bend is what drew so many people. It was a beautiful land, some of God's finest work. Bear Mountain sloped upward, its surface covered with woodlands.

The marsh grasses that grew along the banks of the Holden River were lush and green, swaying slightly in the summer breeze. The open meadows were a haven for various birds and insects. Rabbits and woodchucks made their home there. Wild blackberries and strawberries grew abundantly in these verdant fields.

It smelled like a little bit of heaven. The fragrance of honeysuckle, lilac, and wild flowers lingered in the summer air. After the settlers began to come in, the occasional fence marked ownership. Graveled pathways led the way between houses. Some less traveled paths meandered through the fields; hunters often used these. Up the mountain side, larger animals wandered. The mountain lion, bobcat, foxes, and wolves lived in the rocks and crevices of Bear Mountain.

Before the industrialization of Kingston, the Holden River boasted the best fishing in Tennessee. It was also a child's place of discovery and enchantment. Those growing up there became adults and sometimes moved away but could never forget the sweetness of the land or the peace of the mountain.

The Eastern Kodax Company was the first factory that would later become the main source of income for many in Porter's Bend. It was also the first factory to dump their chemical waste into the Holden River. The once-clean clear waters became a murky pond. This effectively limited the once-thriving river life of the Holden.

The smell from the factory's smokestacks adulterated the flowery smell of the meadows. Those familiar with the land before the rise of such things hated what it did to the land. Those that came afterward accepted it and knew no difference.

Thus is progress, good or bad. John and Bessy Small were just one of the families that settled in the Bend. It was a warm spring day that Fanny Small came into the world. John Small, the father, paced up and down in front of the cabin he shared with his beloved wife. His sister-in-law was with his wife, assisting with the birth. His brother George was with him, leaning against a tree, watching John. The sound of a woman's agonizing screams ripped through the otherwise serene outdoors, a stark contrast to the clear blue sky.

"Why was this taking so long?' John thought anxiously. She had been so uncomfortable this last month. What if something was wrong? What would he do? No, he mustn't allow himself to think those thoughts. Still, it had been twenty hours since she went into labor. The hours dragged by with every minute an eternity to the overwrought husband.

The screaming had subsided the last half hour. George sat by this time, smoking a pipe. Anna appeared at the door of the cabin. Her face belied the telltale truth before she could utter any words.

"Come and see your daughter," she told John. He ran to the door, trying to see around Anna. "John…" Anna blocked his view with her own body. "Bessy…she's gone, John."

The husband stepped backward, his hands raised, shock making his face turn pale. The hands became clenched into fists, and he beat the warm air around himself, almost as if waging a private rant against the forces that had taken all he had ever lived for or wanted.

"You have a daughter," Anna said in a calm, stoic manner.

His hands collapsed to his sides, defeated. He entered the cabin. The child lay swaddled in a small blanket next to his dead wife's body. John walked to the edge of the bed and beheld his child's face. The little thing seemed rodent-like to him, not human. It moved its small fists and proceeded to stick them into its mouth. *Strange-looking thing*, his mind thought. Something akin to anger, resentment, and feelings he didn't know he was capable of began to seethe through him. He walked away, quickly, to the door opening. He retched.

"John?" George was beside him, "ya gonna be all right?" his brother queried, not sure what the right thing to say was just now.

"Get rid of it," John spat out, still sick.

"What?" George was puzzled.

"I don't want it, that THING in there. It's not a child, it's a demon. It killed my Bessy!" John's voice broke at this last, and he collapsed, in a heap, outside the cabin.

George and Anna exchanged a look. A silent understanding between them; the two of them needed no words. *It would take time for this open wound to heal,* she thought. Anna went back inside, wrapped the baby more tightly with the blanket. She began the walk home through the trees. George stayed to dig the grave.

3

George and Anna

Anna had always wished for a little girl. She and George had two boys, Jimmy and Paul, ages seven and five. They might have tried to have a baby girl, but now…would John get over his aversion to his daughter when time made the loss of Bessy a little bearable? She sighed. Time would tell, she thought to herself. Only time would tell.

For the present, she could revel in having an infant girl to care for and love. It was easy for George and Anna to love the child. Anna suggested the name Fanny, after her own mother. George agreed it was a fine name. Fanny seldom cried. She fussed somewhat if she was hungry or wet. Otherwise, she was angelic. She focused on Anna intently during feeding times or when she held her and rocked her in front of the hearth.

Anna fed the child a mixture of cow's milk with the cream still on top, adding honey to sweeten it. One early spring morning, Anna placed a nipple, fashioned from an old hot water bottle, between the tiny pink lips. Fanny's mouth seemed to spread into what looked like a toothless smile as she gazed at Anna. It was something of a comical sight, and Anna let out a delighted laugh. George awoke and idled sleepily in to see what was so funny. Anna, still laughing, told him what had just transpired.

"Oh, she probably has gas," he told her.

"No, she doesn't," his wife insisted. "She smiled at me!"

◆———————◆

Fanny grew at a rate that exceeded both of George and Anna's sons. Anna was kept busy making new clothes to accommodate each growth spurt. She had started out with the boy's nightgowns, but as Fanny grew, Anna wanted everyone to know she was a little girl. She made dresses decorated with flowers and ruffles. George watched and was content knowing Anna had the little girl she had always wanted. It was a shame John had no love for his own daughter, he thought, but was glad for Anna's sake.

George's only concern for Fanny was...the little one just wasn't exactly cute. For one thing, she had been born with a lazy eye. Some folks around these parts were so superstitious they were bound to make up silly stories. He told Anna it didn't matter. He was certain she would outgrow any awkwardness she had now and turn into a beautiful woman. Even if she didn't, she would always be beautiful to them.

He loved to watch Anna care for Fanny. Bathing and feeding her, rocking her to sleep. It made him remember the day he first laid eyes on his wife.

He met Anna Lightner one summer when he worked for a neighboring farmer, helping to get the crops planted. Later, at harvest time, he would help with that as well. Anna was the farmer's niece and was visiting from up north with her mother.

On a hot day, while George was working in the fields, the heat of the sun was beating down upon him. Farmer Palmer called out, "Anna!" George glanced over his shoulder to see who his employer was calling to. He saw a young girl walking toward them. Her hair was long and the color of the sun. She carried a jug of lemonade. George thought he had never laid eyes on anything so lovely as this golden-haired girl.

He took the jug after Farmer Palmer had drunk from it and gulped down half of the jug's content. Anna laughed at how quickly he drank the cold lemonade. George thought her laughter sounded like the tinkling of silver bells. It was the sweetest of sounds to his ear. He was smitten from that moment on.

By harvest time, he knew he wanted Anna to be his wife. He could tell she liked him as well. They married the following spring. Farmer Palmer knew George was a good man but regretted losing a good farm hand.

They came to Porter's Bend since his brother, John, lived there. They had a good life these past years. He thanked God always for all the blessings He had bestowed upon him and his family.

4

Church

The first Baptist Church of Porter's Bend was a white clapboard building with hand-made benches that served as the pews. Years earlier, the church had started out in the same spot with folks sitting on blankets and using tree stumps for chairs. Later, God graciously provided the community with a building for everyone who wanted to come, confess their sins, and praise and worship God.

The worship style of this church was a cross between true Baptist and Pentecostal with shades of holiness tossed in the mix. No matter the style of worship, the hearts of the folks in the church were full of love for God and Jesus and for their fellow man.

George and Anna took their sons to church from the time they were tiny babies. They did the same with Fanny. As Fanny grew from an infant to a lively toddler, she was well acquainted with the sights, sounds, and even the smells of the local church. It was not unusual to see the little girl sitting beneath the pew playing with a toy; it was usually a rag doll or a home-made stuffed animal.

It was only after the age of accountability children were expected to sit in a pew to listen and respond to the service. The age of accountability was often disputed among the members of the congregation. Some said it was when the child could read the Bible. Still others claimed it was at the age of thirteen. Thirteen being when hormones began coursing through young bodies leading to temptation and, inevitably, sin. And there were those who believed it was different with each individual child, depending on their level of maturity.

George and Anna had agreed it was the latter. Their oldest son, Jimmy, had been saved at the youthful age of five. Paul was now five but still had problems sitting through a worship service without squirming or falling asleep. As such, his mother allowed Paul to play with Fanny and keep her occupied while both parents praised and prayed and listened to the word of the Lord.

There were several preachers who graced the pulpit. The main gentleman, considered the pastor of the church, was Isaiah Tucker. He was a fellow of thirtyish years whose hair was already turning gray. (Aunt Anna said it was the stress of looking after all the church folks and their many spiritual needs that caused him to be prematurely gray.) Pastor Tucker started out his preaching low of voice, and over a period of ten or fifteen minutes, his words gave way to a decibel level that left him without the ability to speak for a day or two. All the preachers were good at getting God's message across to sinners punctuating what was said with pulpit pounding, altar jumping, and sometimes "falling out" in the Holy Ghost. It was a glorious and happy gathering when the church doors were open.

There were several churches in Porter's Bend. There was Methodist, Lutheran, and a Church of the Brethren. Aunt Anna told Fanny that the Baptist church was the only one that preached the entire word of the Lord. Fanny accepted her aunt's pronouncement as she believed everything her aunt ever told her. Aunt Anna never told a lie. Fanny did notice that when her family gathered for church on a Sunday, they arrived earlier than any of their counterparts and also dismissed services long after the Methodists, Lutherans, and the Brethren had since departed home for dinner. It was not uncommon for Fanny's stomach to be heard growling during the last prayer.

For Fanny, having grown up in the church, it became like a second home to her. The sound of a preacher's impassioned cry for lost souls, the music, handclapping, and the lilting sounds of folks speaking in tongues were second nature to Fanny. When someone new and unfamiliar with the loud, enthusiastic worship service jumped in their seat when a preacher pounded his fist, Fanny couldn't help but giggle to herself. She knew every hymn from memory, and she believed in the Bible as God's holy word.

Seven-year-old Fanny sat on the wooden church bench beside her brother, Jimmy. Her short legs dangled over the edge of the seat, her feet too high to even touch the old wooden floor. It was not Pastor Tucker speaking that evening. It was a guest speaker. Fanny had overheard two ladies call him, somewhat disdainfully, "Preacher Clarkson." They said that he was not a good preacher because he stood before the congregation and preached with a pack of cigarettes in his shirt pocket. This "habit" made him a target of controversy. Many thought smoking was a sin that could keep you from entering heaven. Still others believed since we are all mere humans, it was only natural to succumb to temptations such as smoking. God didn't approve, but it was not necessarily a sin. Fanny wondered how grown-up folks figured all this stuff out.

It was summer in Porter's Bend at the time. On a very hot and muggy August evening, Fanny and her family occupied their usual pew in the Baptist Church. The windows were all open, but that did little to diminish the heat that seemed to permeate the church folks' very pores. The night was clear, boasting what seemed like a million stars, lighting the pathway for all lost souls to the little church house. A revival was going full scale that particular evening, so that the pews were full and folks. Some stood in the back behind the pews as well. They had come from miles around to hear the litany of preachers try to out-preach one another.

Fanny was listening, but the words didn't really penetrate her mind. It was sort of like when Aunt Anna talked about the correct way to clean the kitchen or the proper way to make a bed. She heard the words, she saw the preacher's mouth moving and his arms gesticulating, but she couldn't comprehend the sounds he made. She almost felt a little sleepy. Soon, Fanny began to sense something else was at work. As she sat there, Fanny began to feel what she could only describe as a "pull," an urging. Struggling to identify where this pull was coming from, Fanny tried to listen to what the preacher was saying. It only seemed to increase the intensity of the pulling, and it was then that she realized, it was urging her to go to the altar. This magnetic pull was incredibly powerful. Even though she gripped the edges of the pew with both her hands, she was having difficulty resisting the pull. She realized she was not afraid; she felt a sense of longing, but she didn't know what she was longing to find. She only knew she *did not* want to go up to that altar. A shy girl by nature, the thought of going up there in front of all these strangers was more terrifying to her than the actual powerful force pulling her out of her seat.

After what seemed like hours, Fanny's resolve was weakening. At last, she stood up, her legs feeling unusually wobbly as if she had run fast for a long distance. She moved forward and couldn't help but notice that her feet did not seem to touch the floor. She didn't dare look down to see if it was true, though, just in case she really *was* floating along. She reached the altar, sometimes called the mourner's bench because souls burdened down with sin came there to mourn and cry out to Jesus.

Fanny knelt, and the moment her knees touched the floor in front of the altar, she began to make involuntary noises. At first, she thought someone else was making the noises. She became suddenly aware *she was the one making the noise!* It seemed to come from somewhere deep inside her, pouring out with the same vehemence she had vomited when she was sick with flu the previous winter. At the same time, she felt like she was being cushioned with pillows on all sides of herself. When she leaned into the pillows, she became silent. She was aware of other people around her. One of her brothers was kneeling next to her, his hand on her shoulder, praying. Others stood all around her, joyfully bringing Fanny to her feet, hugging her with laughter and "God bless you, child!" and other joyful phrases. It seemed as though she was being congratulated, but she had no idea what she was being praised for doing. It was all very confusing. She realized with substantial relief that she no longer experienced any strange pulling or any other odd feelings. And so it was, with great fanfare, that she walked out of the church house with her hand in Aunt Anna's, that the family headed back home for the remainder of the evening. Fanny had been saved!

The following day, Fanny thought it must have had a dream. That was until Aunt Anna chastised her for getting up late. "You have a reputation to live up to now," she had said in a tone that indicated Fanny knew what her aunt was talking about. Fanny knew then what she remembered was no dream her mind might have conjured up during hours of sleep. It had really happened. Everyone took it for granted that Fanny understood what happened and didn't find it necessary to explain.

After considerable pondering over the events of that evening, Fanny came up with the answer for herself. She had been saved by Jesus! She did wonder why it was called being saved. Her aunt explained it to her upon asking; it is because we are each saved from the fires of hell by accepting Jesus as our savior. Fanny did not want to appear ungrateful to Jesus. So she thanked him for her salvation and asked him, in childlike innocence, why couldn't he have made her just a little bit pretty while he was at it.

5

Fanny's First Year of School

John Small, once a vibrant man, had become a quiet, unhappy man. His brother, George, didn't know how to help him. He and Anna included John in their daily prayers, of course. They knew God was working on it, but whatever God was doing in John's life seemed to move very slowly.

Since his daughter's birth seven years earlier, John had become withdrawn. One might say he became something of a hermit. He seldom left his cabin, and the once-plowed fields he owned lay dormant. He seemed happy enough when George came around, but otherwise, he seemed to have no pleasure in his life.

In regard to his daughter, Fanny, he wanted nothing to do with her. He had actually convinced himself that she was his wife's killer. He acted as if she were sent deliberately to steal his very happiness. The inability to forgive his only daughter, a bitter burden, took over his life. What should have been loved, he hated; what should have been cherished, he ignored.

The occasional rabbit or squirrel gave John a means to eat, that is, when he could rouse himself to go hunting. George and Anna invited him for meals and had told John their door was always open. They urged him to come to visit often, hoping that his heart would soften toward Fanny. That didn't seem to be happening any time soon. George and Anna tried to be understanding; they knew they couldn't judge John for his atypical emotions.

On a September afternoon, John arrived at his brother's home to share dinner at their table. George tried to make small talk once the family was seated.

"So, John, how has the hunting been this summer?" he inquired.

Barely glancing up, John replied, "All right, I guess."

George cleared his throat and said, "Jimmy is going to be helping full-time this season getting in the crop, aren't you, son?"

Jimmy saw that his father was steering the conversation toward each of the children and responded with, "Yes, Father."

George continued by saying, "Paul, what are you looking forward to in school this year?"

Paul grimaced somewhat and said, "I'm not. I wish I could stay home and help like Jimmy."

George and Anna chuckled lightly at this comment from their youngest son.

Anna ventured, "Fanny is starting school too, you know."

John looked up then. He looked directly at Fanny. The child sat next to Anna and Paul sat on her other side. She'd been respectfully quiet, but hearing her name mentioned, she stopped chewing, swallowed her food, and smiled.

Over the past seven years of Fanny's young life, she had come into contact with John Small many times. She had been told he was her real father, although she wasn't sure just what that meant. She always tried her hardest to be good when he was around. She was quiet, never speaking unless spoken to. She had become accustomed to his attitude. It didn't make his words any easier to hear, however. He told her she was ugly, and she knew he was right. She had heard her aunt and uncle talk about it. He said she was stupid, and she believed that as well. He said other things too. Fanny did not always understand, but she knew her father was probably right about whatever he said. Whenever she was near her father, Fanny felt an ache in her chest. It made her want to cry, but she didn't know why. No one else had this effect on her.

"What are you smilin' about?" John asked her in a sarcastic tone.

"Noth…nothing, sir." Fanny sat and stared back at her father, feeling small, even while sitting by Aunt Anna.

"School won't help that one," John said in disgust. "She's an evil one, that one."

"John," said Anna sternly, "I'll thank you not to talk that way. She's just a child, for heaven's sake! She's not any such thing as you say. Why, she's been saved and baptized!"

"Hrmph!" John grunted. "There's no salvation for that one," he continued.

"Fanny, honey," Uncle George said kindly to his niece, "why don't you go play with your dolly in your room."

Fanny obediently left her chair, walking away to her bedroom. "Yes, sir," she said, her tiny voice trembling with the tears she was fighting to hold back.

When the child was out of the room, George said to his brother, "What is wrong with you, John? I know you miss Bessy, but it has been seven years now. You can't talk to that little girl like that, especially in her own home. If you can't control yourself, you can't come here anymore. That's just how it has to be." George's tone was firm. He loved his brother and tried to be understanding, but he just couldn't bear to see that painful expression in Fanny's eyes.

"Hrmph," John grunted again, "fine." With that, he pushed his chair away from the table, rose, and walked out. Anna and George exchanged anxious looks between one another. Jimmy and Paul sat in stunned silence. This was partly because of their Uncle John's harsh words to their cousin and partly because they had *never* heard their father tell anyone they weren't welcome in their home.

"Boys," Anna said softly, "go to your room, please."

George and Anna sat together, holding hands, praying together, for the next hour.

Jimmy was fourteen. He was now going to be his father's right-hand man on the farm. This was standard practice for folks around these parts. He could read and write enough to get through life, and now, he would learn to farm.

Paul would go to school until he was thirteen also and follow in his father's chosen profession as well.

With Fanny, things would be different. Girls were expected to marry and start a family of their own. George and Anna would make sure she met the right sort of young man and steer her in the right direction. They believed that God would guide them in this regard, just as he had in their own lives.

Some girls married as young as thirteen or fourteen and had children too. George and Anna had some concerns because Fanny was not the prettiest little girl. The lazy eye made her even less appealing. They hoped she would be more comely in a few years. Perhaps she would blossom into a lovely young girl.

Fanny was a quiet spirit. This was in sharp contrast to her rough and tumble cousins. She entertained herself with her dolls and genuinely enjoyed helping out on the farm or in the kitchen with her aunt. They couldn't have asked for a better child than Fanny.

Now, summer was coming to an end. Fanny knew the song of the locust hailed the advent of the fall season. Prior to this year, she gladly had anticipated all that came with the changing colors of the leaves, the cool, crisp mornings, and the preparations for the upcoming holidays. This time, though, was very different. Fanny had to begin school.

Each passing day brought on the fear of being separated from Uncle and Auntie.

"What if no one likes me, Auntie?"

Her aunt's face softened as she said, "Everyone will love you, honey." That being said, Anna did harbor some fear that Fanny might be teased over the lazy eye.

The dreaded first day arrived. Paul was up and out the door early, running down the path that led to school. He was happy to go to play with his friends. They would throw a ball around the school yard until the teacher rang the bell.

Fanny dawdled, hoping to put off the inevitable. "Auntie?" she questioned, while putting on her stockings.

"Yes, child?" Anna tried to answer patiently. She was trying to comb Fanny's hair while she was doing this. If she didn't, Fanny's slow meandering would make her late.

"I feel sick to my stomach," the little girl whimpered. Fanny had prayed to God that morning and asked him to help her not to have to go to school. Was this his plan? she wondered.

"You'll feel better after you eat some breakfast." Anna was sure Fanny was saying this so she could stay at home, so she blithely glossed over Fanny's stomach problems.

Finally, dressed and having eaten her breakfast, there was just enough time to get Fanny down the path to the school house. The knot in Fanny's tummy tightened with each step she took toward the dreaded place. Aunt Anna chattered away about the beauty of the mountain with its autumn colors flaming and the fun they would have at when they made the apple butter later that month. Fanny heard what her aunt was saying, but her own anxiety kept her from commenting.

They continued until the laughter of the other children was heard and the school house was in full view. "Here we are, Fanny! Aren't you excited?"

Fanny swallowed hard, and holding her aunt's hand, she walked across the threshold of the classroom. That's when it happened. It came forth with such force that it even spattered the hem of her aunt's dress. It covered Fanny's front and the floor directly in the spot where she stood, vomit covered and embarrassed. Fanny cried then. She felt the big, hot tears coursing down her cheeks. The chunks of her undigested breakfast adorned her Sunday dress and the tops of her new Mary Janes.

The teacher, Mr. Barkley, found a towel and ran over to the two of them. He bent over to clean the floor. "Auntie, I'm…" sobs choked Fanny's words, "I'm sorrrrrry."

The kindly teacher smiled and said, "Nothing to worry about, dear." Anna attempted to help with the mess.

"Why don't you take her back home for today?" Mr. Barkley said. "Tomorrow will be a better day." Anna nodded, and she and Fanny walked, silently, down the path toward home.

6

Girl in the Mirror

She may have been young by years, but Fanny was an old soul. She was very self-conscious, especially about her appearance.

A reflection gazed back from the bedroom mirror. The mirror sat atop a grand old dresser that her aunt's mother had brought over from "the old country." Fanny asked her aunt where the old country was she learned it was Belgium. She imagined what it must have been like to live there, far across the ocean. Aunt Anna showed Fanny a picture of herself wearing a Dutch hat; a white material that covered the head closely with two ends on each side turned upward. The girl in the picture had also worn shoes carved out of wood. She thought to herself that those shoes must have hurt the girl's feet.

Fanny heaved a heavy sigh thinking to herself, "Why couldn't God have made me pretty?" Well, she thought to herself, at least her nose wasn't too big. One of the other girls at school had a big nose with a bit of a hook on the end of it. The other children called the big nosed girl names that would have certainly made anyone cry.

Her cheekbones were high and her mouth was small, her lips thin. The crossed eyes were the one thing Fanny found almost unbearable. Like the girl whose nose was too large for her face, many were the nicknames she had to endure because of her right eye. The muscle that was supposed to hold her eye in place was weak on one side and so the iris was not centered like the other eye. The cruel nature of these names caused her heart to ache and her eyes to sting with hot tears. Just thinking about it made her tear up. She hastily wiped the moisture from her face. At least she had nice hair. It matched her eyes. Not that anyone ever noticed *that*.

Fanny brushed her long brown hair that had auburn streaks through it and tied it into a pony tail with a ribbon that matched her dress. She picked up her Bible. It was just the right size for her small hands and it had a white cover with gold lettering on the front that spelled "Holy Bible." It had been a gift from Uncle George and Aunt Anna after Fanny accepted Jesus as her savoir. Jesus was the one who got her through the name-calling and the teasing. She prayed every night to Him, kneeling by her bedside, hands clasped tightly and eyes squeezed shut. "Please, please, please, Jesus, make my eyes uncrossed so no one will make fun of me anymore." It had been her consistent plea since

Fanny began first grade. That, and for Gunilla Gotlieb's family to move far away.

Gunilla was a girl who targeted Fanny as an easy mark. It had been Gunilla that enticed and encouraged all the other children to pick on her. She was also a head taller than all the other girls. She wore her blond hair in braids that hung like fat sausages on either side of her face. She wore bib overalls like some of the boys did. If it had not been for the braids, Gunilla could have easily passed for a boy.

Fanny picked up her Bible and turned to Psalms. She read chapter 23. The twenty-third Psalm was her favorite, and it spoke to Fanny in a special way; she felt like Jesus was letting her know He was looking out for her no matter what. Fanny wanted to do what would be pleasing to Jesus in the face of her tormentors. So she dutifully asked Him to enable her to forgive Gunilla for being so mean. But it wasn't easy.

She turned to her aunt for advice with her troubles. "Auntie, what can I do to make Gunilla stop being so mean to me?" Fanny asked one quiet evening while she put away dishes.

"Do you speak to the child when you see her at school… before class starts, I mean?" Aunt Anna asked her.

"No, I try not to attract her attention," she said, somewhat sourly.

"Well, then, why don't you try it?" She looked at Aunt Anna as if her aunt was crazy.

"She'll just say or do something mean to me!" Fanny declared. "She hates me, Auntie."

"I doubt she hates you. You don't know her well enough to make that call. Try doing something nice for her. It's awfully hard to be mean to someone when they've been nice to you."

"I guess…" Fanny sounded doubtful. *It might not hurt to try though. Or it just might!* she thought to herself.

The school year was only a couple of months along. Fanny didn't know if she could last until the holidays when all the students got a break for the first time during the school year. She looked up to the ceiling, envisioning the gates of heaven beyond it, and said, "Jesus, please help me to get through every day until then." And with that, Fanny went out of her bedroom to begin the day at school.

7

Love Works a Miracle

After giving her aunt's remarks thoughtful pondering, Fanny decided she should do something that Gunilla wouldn't expect her to do. She thought she should make sure she said "good morning" when she saw her at school. Fanny gave a lot of thought to this challenge. She didn't want to do anything that came across as being fake or phony. It had to be a sincere gesture. She prayed that God would guide her in this endeavor. The more she thought about it, the greater the desire became to do a kind and loving act for Gunilla. She remembered how just a few short hours ago, she had been gripped with fear of this girl, but now, she felt this tremendous surge of kindness motivating her. Fanny owned a small Bible with a white cover given to her by Aunt Anna. Now, the scripture came to her mind: "Perfect love casts out all fear." Surely God was giving her His ability to love and look past hurtful words and actions. She realized God was entrusting her with a great duty; the duty all Christians must embrace. To love one another as we love ourselves. She prayed for strength to carry out this mission.

Then, an idea came to her. Fanny loved books. Perhaps she could share this love of books with Gunilla. Mr. Barkly had given Fanny a copy of *The Wizard of Oz* by E.B. White. It was absolutely her favorite book, and she had read it many times over. When she imagined the look of surprise and happiness on Gunilla's face, she couldn't help but smile herself.

When would be the right time? The sun had not yet set over Bear Mountain. At six o'clock, most families would be sitting down to supper, but if Fanny wanted to do this good deed, she would need to leave right now in order to get back home before dark.

Her aunt was getting ready for Uncle George to come in for supper, but Fanny *had* to leave now. She explained that she knew what God wanted her to do and it couldn't be put off. Aunt Anna reluctantly agreed Fanny could go, but to mind she was to be home before darkness arrived. Reassuring her aunt, Fanny put on her sweater as the air was quite chilly with a breeze coming down from the mountain.

The Gotlieb's farmhouse was a little more than a mile from the Small's house. If she hurried, she could probably walk the distance in fifteen minutes. As she walked, her mind began to conjure up images of Gunilla not receiving the gift in the spirit Fanny intended; what if she was angry and told her to get out? Fanny pushed these thoughts aside, thinking surely with Gunilla's family present, she would be on her best behavior. At any rate, she knew she was doing what the Lord wanted her to do, so whatever transpired, she could get through it with His help.

She softly knocked on the front door, hoping she would not need to knock a second time. She didn't want to delay the errand she had set out to accomplish. No need to fear, the door swung open wide, and in the doorway stood a tall, heavyset woman whose blond hair was streaked with gray. An apron was tied around the woman's waist, and flour dusted her face and hands. It appeared Fanny had interrupted dinner preparations. A moment passed in which Fanny tried to ask for Gunilla, but no words were forthcoming. The harried woman asked her what she wanted rather impatiently, and Fanny gathered her presence of mind to inquire after Gunilla.

The woman, turned and strode back into the house leaving the door open for Fanny to follow her. Fanny gingerly stepped in, and Mrs. Gotlieb gestured toward another room and went quickly back to her work station.

The doorway was covered with a flowered curtain. Fanny pushed the curtain aside and saw into the room that looked as though it was used as a parlor. On one side, Gunilla was sitting on a settee. Next to her was a boy, of indeterminate age. He sat in an odd kind of chair; it was fashioned with a tall back with arms attached on either side. It was been painted black. The oddest part of it was the foot pedals on which the boy rested each foot and the large wheels on each side of the chair. There were cushions that looked as though each was made from a quilt material on the back, arms, and seat. Fanny thought Mrs. Gotlieb had probably made them. A small tray was positioned in the front. The boy's thin arms lay idly on top the tray.

He was wearing overalls and a flannel shirt. The legs of the overalls seemed almost flat as if they were empty. In fact, if not for the spindly ankles poking out the hem of each pant leg, Fanny wouldn't have believed the boy had any legs at all. His arms were not much larger than his ankles, and his head lolled to one side as though his neck was unable to hold it upright. The boy's hands were held at odd angles. Fanny had not ever seen anyone in such a condition. Each hand was in the form of a half clasped fist. Gunilla had been feeding him, and she wiped the boy's mouth as some food dripped down his chin.

Gunilla did not notice her visitor at first. When she saw Fanny standing there by the curtained doorway, she blushed, embarrassed. Without her usual menacing attitude, she asked in a low tone, "Why are you here?"

"I wanted to say I am sorry," Fanny said softly. "I brought you a present," she offered the book to the other girl.

"Sorry for what?" Gunilla sounded suspicious.

Fanny reminded her about the cigar box incident involving Ben. Fanny told her she didn't know why things happened as they had, but anyway, she was very sorry.

Gunilla merely shrugged her shoulders as she put another spoonful of mashed potatoes to the boy's lips.

Fanny showed her the book she brought and laid it on the settee, next to her. She told Gunilla it was her personal favorite and she thought Gunilla would probably like it as much as she had. Gunilla stared at Fanny as if she had suddenly grown a tail or some such thing.

Fanny stood by the doorway for what seemed like hours, saying nothing. After several minutes, Gunilla began to speak. She told Fanny that the boy was her older brother. When he was about six years old, he suffered a seizure. The doctor where they lived at that time didn't know what had happened to him or why. Little by little, he lost the ability to walk, then his arms became paralyzed as well. He lost all muscle tone. For as long as Gunilla could remember, she had helped to take care of him. Her father had built the chair for him so he could be wheeled from one place to another.

When her three older brothers eventually left home, only Gunilla and her one sister remained. It wasn't long after her brothers left to marry and lead their own lives that her sister got married also and left home. Now, only Gunilla and her mother were left to take care of her disabled brother. Gunilla said his name was Gunther. Her mother had to take care of the house, cook meals, and help her father with the chores. Gunilla had to bathe and feed Gunther, and she sat with him quite often so he was not alone. Her parents worried he might injure himself somehow if he was left alone unattended.

Fanny couldn't imagine a girl only three years older than herself having this tremendous responsibility. Aunt Anna and Uncle George had chores assigned to her and her brothers, but nothing so consuming as Gunilla faced. No wonder she seemed angry all the time.

Gunilla seemed to read Fanny's thoughts and said she didn't mind taking care of her brother. She was his sister, and it was only right. Her mother couldn't do it all alone. She said she wished she didn't have to go to school though because she'd be able to help her mother out more with Gunther.

Fanny was surprised. It had never occurred to her that someone might not enjoy school as much as she did.

"Don't you like learning new things?" she asked.

"Why? I don't read very good anyhow, so why bother? Reading and the rest of it is not going to help my brother." Gunilla said this with resignation.

Fanny just nodded slowly as though she agreed with her. Her sympathetic nature made her heart ache for Gunilla, her brother, and her mother. She couldn't find any comforting words that sounded right, so she kept silent. When Gunilla seemed have finished telling the story of her family, Fanny stood up to leave. Gunilla did not turn her head away from her brother or say good-bye. Fanny said softly that she had to get home before dark and she quickly left. Everything seemed so sad and hopeless, Fanny feared she might cry.

Fanny now knew why Gunilla learned how to stand up for herself. She didn't *want* to be a bully, but she wasn't going to let anyone push her around. She admitted to liking Brad, but she knew he wouldn't ever pay any attention to her. She had tried to take it out on Fanny although she knew it wasn't her fault.

Fanny felt what seemed like real physical pain around her heart as she realized Gunilla had been like this because it was easier than dealing with the pain and unfairness of her brother's illness. The responsibility of caring for him in the mornings before walking to school, the time she spent with him afterward, until her father came in and put him to bed had become like a heavy load. It was no wonder Gunilla didn't get her homework done; she spent all her free time caring for Gunther.

Fanny made up her mind to tell Gunilla she could help her learn to read better. If she could accomplish this, she might try harder in school. She prayed for the girl she had been terrified of only a couple of days ago and asked God to help her.

8

A Good Neighbor

Fall was almost over. Uncle George, as all farmers in Portage Bend, was busy gathering in the farm's crops. The night air became cooler and the days crisper with the promise of winter close at hand.

The change in the weather was causing some folks to fall ill. The congregation had been noticeably smaller the past Sunday. Mrs. Gotlieb had been one of those to become sick. She was bedbound with the croup. Since they were the nearest neighbors to the Small's, Anna Small took it upon her shoulders to care for the Gotlieb children and prepare the meals while their mother was ailing.

Aunt Anna called Fanny to rise early that morning. She fixed breakfast for Uncle George, and the two of them set out for the Gotlieb's farmhouse. It was a bright sun-filled morning with a distinct chill that set Fanny's teeth to chattering. Fanny had begged for a reprieve, saying she could have gotten Uncle George's breakfast so Aunt Anna could have gotten an earlier start. Her aunt was not giving into any of Fanny's excuses.

Upon their arrival, the Gotlieb door was opened by Henry, the oldest son of Heinrich and Elsa Gotlieb. The Gotliebs were second generation Swedes whose parents had met on the boat coming to America over sixty some years ago. Henry was a tall blond-haired fellow with muscular shoulders and massive arms earned by bailing and tossing one-hundred-pound bundles of hay and alfalfa. His blue eyes expressed the gratitude he proclaimed to Aunt Anna. "So kind of you, Mrs, Small. My family is indebted to you for your assistance to us." Henry said as he motioned for them to enter.

Elsa, although ill, tried bravely to get up, but without success. Aunt Anna gently admonished the woman back into bed, pulling the comforter around her stout shoulders. Heinrich Gotlieb coughed as he put on his overcoat to begin the day's work. Aunt Anna warned him he should stay in and take care of himself lest his coughing become the croup. A stubborn man, Mr. Gotlieb thanked Aunt Anna for her concern but headed out the door.

Anna got Fanny to go set the kitchen table while she began working on the breakfast. Fanny did not see Gunilla. She had only saw Henry when she and her aunt arrived. Henry had married a few years earlier but was present today to help his father with the harvesting as he did each year. Perhaps Gunilla was getting ready for school, she thought to herself. When the food was ready, Aunt Anna told her to call Gunilla, and her aunt rang the bell on the front porch summoning the men from the fields.

Fanny walked quietly to the curtained doorway and peeked into the parlor. There was Gunilla with Gunther. She was buttoning his shirt and didn't see Fanny. Gunilla tickled Gunther under his chin, and they both laughed a bit. When Gunilla turned, she saw Fanny and nodded ever so slightly to acknowledge her. Fanny was feeling a little awkward having just witnessed an intimate moment between the siblings. She felt as if it had not been intended for her eyes. Gunilla said, "Could you bring me a plate of food from the kitchen? I'd like to feed my brother."

Fanny told the girl, "Of course I will."

After setting the table as instructed, Fanny thought about Gunilla's poor brother, Gunther. She walked over to her aunt's side and asked softly, "Did you know that Gunilla has a crippled brother?"

"Of course. We've been neighbors since before he was born," Aunt Anna said this as if she thought Fanny had known this.

"How old is he?"

"Well, let's see," her aunt ruminated on the question, trying to tie events together so she could count the years since Elsa had given birth to her disabled son.

"I guess, it's been almost fifteen years now," she said, shaking her head in wonderment at how quickly the time had passed.

"Gunilla would like a plate of food so she can feed him in the sitting room," Fanny suddenly remembered the request.

"What!" Aunt Anna exclaimed," Well, Gunther can eat at the table with the rest of us!"

"Well...," Fanny said slowly, "she asked me to get it for her."

"You just tell her," her aunt declared, "she can bring him out to the kitchen. Imagine, eating in the sitting room."

"But," Fanny interrupted, "if that's how she is used to doing it, should we try to make them do something else?"

"No one should eat in the sitting room." Aunt Anna was firm.

Reluctantly, Fanny went back to the room where Gunilla waited with her brother.

She took a deep breath and said, "My aunt says you must bring Gunther to the table to eat," she said softly. Fanny waited, expecting to be rebuffed.

Without comment, Gunilla went behind her brother's chair and pushed him through the doorway while Fanny held back the curtain.

Aunt Anna smiled at both children as they entered the kitchen.

"Good Morning, children!" she cheerfully sang.

"Good morning, Mrs. Small," Gunilla said, "it's most kind of you to come and help us."

49

"The good Lord wouldn't have it any other way nor would I," Aunt Anna set out plates of steaming eggs, bacon, and biscuits in front of each child.

"That's all right, ma'am," Gunilla pushed aside the proffered plate, "I'll eat mine later. I have to feed Gunther first."

"Nonsense," Aunt Anna said, in a tone so as not to be argued with, "*I* will feed Gunther while everyone eats. You need to get ready for school."

"Well…" Gunilla started to say something, but the firm set face Aunt Anna wore made her stop. "Thank you, Mrs. Small." She pulled the plate of food front of herself and began to eat the food while it was still hot.

Gunther had been quiet during this whole time but surprised everyone when he asked, "Whas wrong wif you eye?" the question was aimed at Fanny, who felt her face flush as the blood coursed upwards. She realized this was the first she had heard Gunther speak.

"It's…it's…," Fanny struggled, not used to having to explain her condition.

"She just has a muscle in that eye that doesn't work the way it's supposed to," her aunt said matter-of-factly.

"My…muscles don work like…their s' poset to eiver," he said, looking at Fanny.

Fanny looked at Gunther shyly who smiled his crooked smile back at her. She smiled in return. Even Gunilla smiled in between bites of her breakfast.

"You are absolutely right," Aunt Anna said in agreement, patting the boy's blond head. At that moment, Mr. Gotlieb and Henry came in the house, red faced from the cold wind. As Mr. Gotlieb stripped off his outwear, he observed Gunther sitting at the table and Anna offering him a spoonful of scrambled eggs.

"Gunilla!" he thundered, "Why is your brother in the kitchen? You know I don't want him to eat at the table!"

Aunt Anna was shocked by Mr. Gotlieb's outburst but didn't think she should tell a father how to take care of his own son. She pressed her lips tightly together to keep from saying something she knew she should not.

"I'm sorry, Papa!" Gunilla started to explain, "It's just that…"

"Don't argue with me. Take him out!" her father demanded. "Now!" he added the last command, assuring Gunilla would have no choice but to comply.

Gunilla did as she was told, pulling the chair back from the table and through the kitchen door back to the sitting room.

Aunt Anna, her eyes wide with dismay, dared not speak.

She rose and served the two men. Fanny and Gunilla left for school moments later.

❖———❖

Anna Small became increasingly agitated, her mind thinking about Mr. Gotlieb's attitude toward his own son. The housework served to calm her as she cleaned the Gotlieb home with a fervor she seldom used. She began to pray, a natural outgrowth of her faith-filled life. When troubled in spirit, turn it over to Jesus, as the old hymn encouraged us to do.

While wielding the mop over the kitchen floor, the thought came to her, "What if Jimmy or Paul had been born with a disability like Gunther Gotlieb?" Anna had to stop mopping momentarily, to consider the question. "Well," she mused to herself, "I would deal with it somehow and not take it out on my child and family."

"Would you be angry?" the inner voice asked. "Do you think you would blame yourself, wondering if you could have prevented it from happening?"

"It's hard to know what I'd do, since I haven't been through that sort of thing," she admitted.

"So it would be fair to say that you are judging this father?" The voice posed an insightful question.

Anna could see she had been at fault feeling angry and judgmental with Mr. Gotlieb. He was probably carrying the weight of the world on his shoulders. She felt great remorse for the man who had hoped for another healthy son only to been given one with a devastating disability. She felt humbled by the blessings she and her husband George enjoyed with the birth of two healthy sons.

The two Gotlieb men returned just prior to lunch. After the meal, Anna asked Mr. Gotlieb if she could speak privately with him. He instructed Henry to resume working and that he would be along shortly.

Anna began slowly, "Come, Heinrich," she said, "sit down and have another cup of coffee."

"What's on your mind, Mrs. Small?" addressing Anna by surname because he was always taught to respect another man's wife by including the husband's name when speaking with her.

"Please understand, I mean no disrespect in what I'm about to say," Anna continued, praying for the right words. "I know it must be very difficult for you, and Elsa also, to deal with a challenge like the one Gunther has. "

Mr. Gotlieb's brows came together, and he opened his mouth to speak, but Anna continued, not seeming to notice, "God gave you this boy, no matter what his condition, to love and care for. Gunther has something to contribute or God would not have given him to you. God makes no mistakes. He only gives us, opportunities to love."

Mr. Gotlieb's face lost the look of anger, and Anna could not, at first, read the face lined with years of hard work and sacrifice.

"I...do...love my boy." His voice choked off, his eyes spilling over with tears. "I...just can't...stand...to see him that way." His shoulders heaved with the force of his sobs.

"You must stop looking at Gunther as a problem and begin to see him as a great blessing," Anna pronounced this, as kindly as she could.

Taking out his handkerchief, Heinrich Gotlieb said, "I know you are right. It is just hard to see my son this way. Knowing he will never walk, never get married, never have what every man has a God given right to enjoy." He wiped his tears away and tried to restore himself. "Mrs. Small, be grateful for what you have. Thank God for healthy sons." He rose and started for the door.

Anna said, "I think it is important that *you* be thankful for *your* son."

He nodded and was out the door to join Henry at work.

Anna bowed her head and said to God, "Thy will be done."

9

A Father's Love

This was the first time Fanny and Gunilla had walked to school together, or anything together, for that matter. After Mr. Gotlieb's angry display at the breakfast table, Fanny didn't know what to say. Or if she should say anything. The first one hundred yards or so passed silently between the two girls.

Then Gunilla said, "It's not that he is angry with Gunther. He is angry with himself."

"But why?" Fanny's natural curiosity compelled her to ask.

"Because he couldn't afford to take mother to a doctor when she was carrying Gunther.

And now, it wouldn't do any good anyway." Gunilla's voice trailed off again into silence.

"What's wrong with him ?" Fanny asked.

"When he was born, the cord was wrapped around his neck. He almost died. And then, my parents noticed, he could hardly move his arms or legs. As he got older, his muscles just didn't seem to grow. He couldn't crawl or walk.

He finally started to talk a little when he was almost five years old."

"Oh," said Fanny, wondering what cord Gunilla was talking about. Since she had no idea how babies are born, she didn't want to appear foolish, so she acted as if she knew exactly what Gunilla was talking about. She would have to ask Aunt Anna later.

"Well, why doesn't he go to school with you?" Fanny asked, innocently.

Gunilla's good behavior toward Fanny was wearing thin. With no adults around to curb her attitude, she turned, exasperated, saying, "Didn't you hear what I said? He's a retard!"

Fanny stopped dead still while Gunilla went marching ahead. In her mind, she wondered what that meant, but she knew she surely wasn't going to ask another question. She walked a ways behind Gunilla the rest of the way to school.

❖———❖

Her father came to dinner that evening. Fanny had sat at the dinner table, eyes downward, looking at her dinner plate the whole time. John Small talked with her aunt and uncle, and only after she asked to be excused did he take any notice of her.

"Finish your food. Money doesn't grow on trees, you know," he had said gruffly. Fanny sat back down, her eyes never moving from her plate. "Well, aren't you going to answer me?" her father nearly shouted. Uncle George and Aunt Anna exchanged a look.

"Yes, sir," Fanny replied softly.

Her aunt said to her father, "Don't force her, John. I think I gave her too much."

"Hmph!" he muttered. "In my day, you didn't get up from the dinner table until you cleaned your plate!"

"There's not much left, "Aunt Anna said, and directing her words to Fanny, said, "Dearie, it's fine, you may be excused."

Fanny stood and left the room quickly before her father had time to make an objection. Fanny hated when her father came to their home. He only came because he felt obligated to Aunt Anna and Uncle George. He didn't have any love for her at all, she felt. Fanny hated her father.

She tried *not* to hate him. She knew Jesus wanted her to love everyone. Why did it have to be so hard? She accepted the fact that he didn't love her, and he, more than likely, never would. She often wondered, how did a father act like that? Oh well, Uncle George and Aunt Anna loved her like she was their daughter. It made the ache she felt in her chest a bit less. Fanny told herself she didn't need him. He was the one person Fanny could not pray for. Her aunt told her that her father was still grieving over the loss of her mother. She said he did love her; it was just hard for him to show it. Fanny did not believe her aunt; she wanted to, but she couldn't.

She had heard him say she was an ugly child. Even if she was, wasn't he still supposed to say she was beautiful? Fanny promised herself that if she ever had children, especially a girl, she would tell her over and over that she was loved and beautiful.

She began her lessons for the next day, but she laid aside the book, unable to concentrate. She would do her homework in the morning. She put on her nightgown, crawled into her bed, trying to still the troubling thoughts with sleep.

10

When the Future Plans Itself

When Fanny walked into the house, Aunt Anna sat in her sewing chair, wiping her eyes with a lace hanky. It was obvious she had been crying.

"Auntie, what's wrong?" Fanny knelt beside her aunt.

Her aunt told Fanny the whole story. "While I was busy today at the church, your brother, Jimmy, came rushing in the door. Jimmy was out of breath having run the entire way. After catching his breath, he related how he and Paul were helping Uncle George load up the wagon to take the crops to Kingston. Jimmy told Paul not to stand so close to the edge of the wagon, but he wasn't paying attention, and sure enough, the horses took a couple steps just as Paul was bending to hoist a bail onto the wagon. Paul fell forward onto the gravel, hitting his head. He just lay there, not moving at all." She paused, to stifle a sob. "Uncle George shouted, "Paul!" and rushed to his side. He laid his head on Paul's chest, pressing his ear against his upper body to see if his heart was still beating. He was able to detect a faint sound. Uncle George picked up Paul and carried him in his arms back here. I told him to put him on our bed since it's downstairs." Anna broke down after saying all this and cried as if her heart was surely broken. Now, Paul lay in the bedroom, looking as though he were merely sleeping. Fanny ran to her bedroom and kneeling, cried out to Jesus, "Jesus, please help my brother get well." She prayed with tears streaming down her cheeks. She spent time thinking of all the good times she had with both of her brothers; they would play games outdoors when the weather was warm. They caught fireflies in a jar with holes punched in the lid, and she remembered how Paul tried to comfort her when the tiny insects eventually died. He had been a good brother, even though she knew Jimmy and Paul were really just cousins. No one could have treated her more like a brother than Jimmy or Paul. And now Paul was hurt, and no one outside of God knew if he would wake up again. She cried and prayed until she fell asleep that night, forgetting to even put on a nightgown. She slept in her school dress that day.

The next morning, Fanny woke early. She realized she had not taken her school dress off but had slept in it. She sat, rubbing her eyes. Suddenly, she remembered the awful events of the prior evening and ran downstairs to her parents' bedroom. She stood in the doorway of the room, noting the bed was all made. It could only mean one thing! Paul woke up and was all better! God had answered her prayer!

She breathed a sigh of relief and ran down the stairs. Aunt Anna stood by the kitchen sink and turned around when Fanny entered the room.

"Aunt Anna," Fanny said, "Paul is all better!"

"Yes, child, your brother is all better." Aunt Anna sounded so solemn. Fanny looked up at her, and there was a certain peace, but sadness as well. Fanny didn't understand. Why did she look so sad, she wondered. And then, as her aunt put her hand to Fanny's face, she knew what had really happened but couldn't wrap her mind around it. Paul had passed from this life into heaven.

"No…no, Aunt Anna, no…" She buried her face in her aunt's body and wondered if she should have asked Jesus to let Paul live instead of just asking Him to make him better. She had asked Him to make Paul better. And she knew Jesus had answered her prayers, just as He always does. Just not the way she wished He would have.

Fanny felt as if she aged that day. She was only seven years old, but she felt as if she had grown up all at once. She had never faced such grief before and thought she might die herself if this pain in her chest did not go away soon. Even the way her father made her hurt did not compare to this kind of pain and sadness. Would it ever go away? Would she ever stop seeing Paul's sweet face, seemingly asleep on the bed, with his eyes shut that would never open again until he reached heaven's gate? Aunt Anna said time would heal the wound; Fanny hoped her aunt was right.

The day Paul was buried was cold and raining. The weather seemed to be mourning right along with the family. Fanny stood, huddled between Uncle George and Aunt Anna with Jimmy pressed close to his father on the other side. Fanny's father was present also. In uncharacteristic generosity of spirit, he offered to have Jimmy and Fanny stay with him for a while until the family recovered sufficiently.

Aunt Anna declined, saying the two children needed to be with them because they were grieving also. Fanny heard her aunt's words with a great sense of relief. It was unthinkable to imagine staying with her father.

After some time passed, Uncle George resumed farming, and Jimmy assisted him as he always had. Aunt Anna went back to her usual routine. Fanny went back to school and lessons. But something had changed. There was no laughter, no excitement before the holidays. A heaviness lay over everything. Time passed, and slowly, the pain became bearable, and the family went back to some sense of normalcy.

The years came and went, and now Fanny was in eighth grade; this would be her last year of school. She wished she could somehow continue, but the only high school was across the river in Kingston. Uncle George and Aunt Anna would not allow her to travel unescorted across the Holden River, and neither of them were able to go each day with her. Other students her age were needed at home or to get an "outside the home" job to help their families make ends meet. So Fanny's dream of continuing school was not to be.

One day, after Fanny had graduated and several months had passed, Uncle George had some disturbing news, which he shared at the dinner table. Fanny's father, John Small, had taken gravely ill and was not expected to live out the month. It was rumored among the folks of Porter's Bend that he had tuberculosis. This was an ailment many folks succumbed to. It was common practice for the people to use their cows for milk; some of these cows had not been tested for the TB infection. Invariably, by the time TB was recognized by the coughing up of blood, it was already too late for an adequate treatment. Fanny, being John Small's only daughter and next of kin, needed to provide care for her father until the time of his death. She would be the heir to all his property at that time.

11

Kingston!

As teenagers, Fanny and Ollie were typical. They loved talking about what they would do as adults. They couldn't wait to experience life for themselves. Ollie, being the bold one of the two, came up with a little plan to get a taste of adventure.

Getting Aunt Anna to agree to let Fanny spend that night and following day at the Reynolds's was so easy, Fanny thought to herself. She felt that little niggling of her conscience. Besides that, she found that she fell easily into telling the lie. Her aunt had not questioned Fanny's motives because she had never given her a reason to doubt her niece. Well, it wasn't Fanny's fault if Aunt Anna was so unreasonable. If she had *asked* her if she could accompany Ollie on the trip to Kingston, surely she would have said "no." Of that fact, there was no doubt. So Fanny was forced to lie, or so she told herself.

Aunt Anna trusted Fanny completely, but she was a little less trusting of Olivia Reynolds. First of all, the Reynolds were Lutheran. To Aunt Anna, that meant they were practically heathens. Olivia seemed too independent for a girl her age. She didn't think the girl's mother kept a close enough eye on her. With Fanny, she did not worry. She was a good girl and would not do anything Anna would not have approved of. She was sure Fanny would not betray her trust.

Fanny told herself that the ends justified the means. She had heard Uncle George use that phrase before, even though she couldn't remember the reason for it, she felt certain this situation applied. She packed her night gown and her best dress. She wanted to look her best for the trip to Kingston. Hugging her aunt and kissing her cheek, she departed to the Reynolds's house.

<hr />

The two friends slept little that night. They laughed and talked into the night. They discussed everything from what hairstyles they liked best to which boys each one of them thought was the handsomest. The morning arrived before Fanny had barely closed her eyes to sleep, or at least, it seemed that way. Both she and Ollie arose and bathed, dressed, and gulped down a breakfast so to begin their adventure. Of course, it was more of an adventure for Fanny than for Ollie.

Mrs. Reynolds thought nothing of Fanny going along with Ollie. She assumed she had gotten permission from her aunt. Vera Reynolds was a single, middle-aged mother.

She had borne Olivia out of wedlock but told folks in Porter's Bend her husband had passed away. It was just easier that way. She didn't need folks looking down their noses at her or Olivia. She kept her daughter, and she was doing her best to raise her right. That ought to count for something, she believed.

Mrs. Reynolds placed the finished dresses in a trunk so Olivia could carry them easily. Thank God she had a natural talent for sewing. She didn't know how they would have been able to get by otherwise. The money from this month's transaction was going to pay next month's rent. She had so many expenses this month she had gotten overextended. But it would all work out, she thought. It always did.

Fanny had twenty-five cents she had saved. Aunt Anna paid her two cents a week for doing the chores. She used three cents of it for fare to cross the river. On the way over, the girls discussed how to spend the day after dropping off the dresses. "What about seeing a picture?" suggested Ollie. Fanny would have loved to do that but didn't want to waste her one day of freedom in the city sitting in a dark theater. Well, they could visit the art museum. It seemed like a good choice; besides, it was free.

Once the dresses were delivered, Ollie asked the shopkeeper for directions to the art museum. It was about twelve blocks away, but rather than spend money on the trolley, they decided to walk and see the sights. Fanny was giddy with the sensation of freedom; she could do what she wanted for the whole day!

"Do you think your aunt suspected anything?" Ollie asked Fanny.

"No, she trusts me," replied Fanny, and again, she felt the sting of her conscience gnawing at her.

The topic was dropped as the girls passed a bakery with wonderful aromas floating out into the September air.

"Let's go in a buy a sweet," Ollie tugged at Fanny's arm, leading her through the door.

"But I only have twenty two cents left, and I'll need three to get back across the river," said Fanny, thinking about the cost.

"Aw, come on, we'll split one," Ollie cajoled Fanny, and with that, they stepped into the bakery. The varieties seemed endless, and both girls had trouble deciding on the same thing. Finally, after going back and forth between two different kinds of delicacy, it was decided they would split a cinnamon bun topped off with a rich icing.

Thanking the clerk for her patience, the two girls continued their journey. They passed some factories, and then the next block housed a grain elevator.

"This must be where Uncle George brings the corn when it's harvested," remarked Fanny.

"Uh huh," answered Ollie, as she ate the last bit of cinnamon bun.

"Wouldn't it be funny if your uncle was here *today*?" laughed Ollie.

"No, it wouldn't be," Fanny said, her tone becoming very serious.

"Oh, silly," teased Ollie, "don't be so scared. No one will see us."

"Well, let's walk faster anyway. I want to get to the museum and see everything," Fanny pulled her hat a little lower, just in case someone did see them, they wouldn't recognize her.

A few more blocks and the museum's sign appeared. The two went in, looking all around at works of art. There were some artifacts from the founding of Kingston too. Fanny read each description the museum had in front of each display, drinking it all in. "Oh, look," remarked Ollie, "there's a guest book."

"Oh," replied Fanny. Both girls perused the names of the previous visitors.

"Should we sign it?" asked Ollie

"Well, I'm sure Aunt Anna and Uncle George will never come in here...so, why not?"

So the girls signed the visitor's log. Fanny wrote her name with big loops with flourish so anyone seeing her signature would think her sophisticated and art savvy.

"Oh, this is so much fun," Fanny gushed.

The museum wasn't large, so they saw all of its contents within an hour's time.

Next, the two decided they were hungry, so they visited a small diner, which seemed the most reasonable choice, money-wise. As the duo sat at one of the tables in the small dining area, they munched happily on sandwiches and pickles.

Fanny had never experienced such a vibrant slice of life. She didn't want it to end, but alas, as all good things do, the time was growing short. They needed to start walking in the direction of the pier to catch the afternoon boat back across the Holden River.

"Ollie, I can't thank you enough for inviting me along today," Fanny said with absolute sincerity.

"Sure," Ollie replied, waving her hand, minimizing the favor.

"You know," began Fanny, "Your mom is so…Well, I guess she's just not as strict as Aunt Anna." She settled on that choice of words because she didn't want to sound as though she was judging Mrs. Reynolds's parenting decisions.

"She says she wants me to be my own woman. Not to have to depend on a man to take care of me," Ollie explained.

"Uncle George and Aunt Anna are afraid I *won't* have a man to take care of me," Fanny said this dolefully.

"How do you feel about that?" Ollie asked her.

"Wow. No one has ever asked me my opinion of the subject. They just assume I'll get married and have a family. Yes, I guess that is what I want too. What else could I do? I'm not pretty like you, Ollie," she said wistfully.

"Fanny," Ollie leaned over as if she was imparting a secret to her, "men don't really care about how a girl looks."

"What?! Yes, they do!" Fanny said, thinking suddenly about Ben Morris.

"No, they don't," Ollie sat back, her arms folded across her chest as though to emphasize her words. "Mom says, 'If you have the right equipment, that's all you need, and the rest is not that important.'"

They both burst into laughter, causing other patrons in the dining area to look at them, wondering what the joke might be. They laughed so hard Fanny's side was aching.

"Oh, Ollie, you are *terrible!*" Fanny managed to say when she was able to speak again. She thought to herself what Aunt Anna would think if she heard the conversation.

Their lunch finished, they proceeded to the pier. It had been the best day of her life thus far. If only it didn't have to be her last, Fanny thought sadly.

12

Wishing and Hoping

Fanny was dejected. The high she felt when she and Olivia were on the sidewalks of Kingston, having the time of their lives, had faded. Now, it seemed like a distant memory. Sitting at the dinner table, she absentmindedly pushed the food around on the plate. Her face showed that her mind was elsewhere.

"What's wrong, Fanny?" Aunt Anna inquired, a worried look caused her brow to furrow.

"Oh…" Fanny was caught off guard. "Nothing…it's just…I guess I'm just tired," she finished, not able to think of any other excuse.

"Well, I certainly hope Vera Reynolds appreciates all the help you must have given her," Aunt Anna commented.

"What?" Fanny had momentarily forgotten about the lie she had told her aunt in order to be allowed to spend the previous Friday night and Saturday at the Reynolds's house.

"She could have offered to give you something," her aunt said.

"Oh, she did offer to," Fanny found herself telling yet another lie. "I told her not to worry about it."

"Fanny, you are too generous for your own good," Aunt Anna said this, while she felt secretly proud of Fanny's attitude. "You should go to sleep a little earlier tonight. You want to be alert for school tomorrow."

"All right," Fanny stood, clearing her plate, preparing to do the dinner dishes.

"I'll get those, dear. You just rest." Aunt Anna's tone was firm.

Fanny nodded and walked to her bedroom. There she thought about the days to come, one running into another, with absolutely nothing for her to look forward to. The tears started to fill her eyes in spite of her best efforts to quell them.

She fell over, face first onto the bed, muffling her agonized sobs so no one else could hear.

Why, why, why? she asked no one in particular. She imagined Jesus, sitting in heaven on his throne, looking down on her with disapproval and shaking his head over her. Is it so wrong to want to experience life beyond the graveled roads and shingled houses of Porter's Bend? If it was, then she was just wrong; she couldn't help but long for something more.

If age were not a barrier, she would go on an epic adventure, she thought to herself while her tears flowed freely. She might even venture into exotic realms like Africa and Europe. She thought it's all no use wishing. Wishing didn't make it so.

Sliding into her nightgown, Fanny finally fell asleep and dreamed of a life in which she did everything she ever wanted to do.

On her walk home from school the next day, Olivia Reynolds came running up beside her. "Wait up, Fanny!" she shouted while she was still a hundred behind her. "Fanny!"

Fanny stopped while Ollie raced up, out of breath, excited to tell her friend what she wanted to say.

Hands on her knees, trying to catch her breath, Ollie said between gasps, "Mom wants me to go back to Kingston next Saturday. Do you wanna come? Please don't say no!" Ollie hopped up and down excitedly, holding onto Fanny's arm as she pleaded with her.

Fanny's first thought response was to scream, "Yes, yes, yes!" but her verbal response was, "I really would love to, but what if I get caught? Aunt Anna would never trust me again." Fanny sighed. "There are other things in life I want to do besides walk around Kingston before I turn twenty-one, you know."

"How could we get caught?" Ollie asked her with a tone of voice that made the possibility of getting caught sound remote.

"I don't know. It just scares me, thinking I might," replied Fanny. "It's okay for *you*, Ollie," Fanny continued, "your mother doesn't care what you do. She wants you to be independent."

"Oh...please, please, please,...it'll be fun!" Ollie would not take no for an answer.

"Well, I'm definitely going to feel out Aunt Anna," Fanny said decidedly, "and if she seems the slightest bit suspicious, I'm not going to risk it."

"That's a good plan," acceded Ollie. "You can let me know on Friday. And if she doesn't want you to stay overnight at my house, we can still go," she finished, smiling.

"Then it's a plan!" Fanny smiled, the possibility of another Saturday exciting her inside.

<hr/>

That evening, over dinner, Fanny brought the subject in what she thought was a nonchalant manner.

"Poor Mr. Reynolds," she began, "Ollie says she has to make ten different styles of dresses by this Friday to keep her consignment job with the dress shop in Kingston."

Fanny did not even mention the possibility of her helping Mrs. Reynolds.

"Well, I wouldn't feel too sorry for her," Aunt Anna replied. "She's fortunate to have a job in this day and time. A lot of folks wish they had jobs like that."

"Sure, I know," Fanny said, looking at her plate. "But you know, she's hardly any time to spend with Ollie, what with all the orders she has. I guess the one I really feel sorry for is Ollie. She's practically raising herself..." Fanny cast a sideways glance to see how her words might be affecting her aunt.

"Ha. That's about right," inserted Jimmy. "The boys at school call her fast...among other things."

"Don't talk about Ollie like that," Fanny said vehemently. "She's my friend, and she's not like that!"

"Yes, Jimmy," chided Aunt Anna, "that kind of talk is just gossip. We don't do that in this household."

"Yes, ma'am," Jimmy said, and when his mother wasn't looking, stuck his tongue out at Fanny.

Fanny's eyes narrowed, hoping that he could see how angry he made her.

Changing her tactics, Fanny said, "Well, I think it would do Ollie a lot of good if I could spend more time with her. You always say, 'Idle hands are the devil's greatest asset.'"

"And what would the two of you be doing? And when were you planning to keep Ollie's hands from idleness?" asked Aunt Anna.

"Well, Saturday would be a good day for us to spend time together," Fanny said this as though she hadn't been thinking about it since her conversation with her friend.

"Hmmm," Aunt Anna replied, "why is it that the one day I could really use some help around here, either Vera Reynolds or Ollie seem to be in desperate need of you?"

"They don't have any relatives around here," Fanny said truthfully. "It's not their fault Ollie's dad died, and they had to move here. I guess I just thought you would *want* me to help someone in need." Fanny shrugged, giving the impression she didn't understand her aunt's objections.

"All right," her aunt relented, "but she can come here."

"But…" Fanny started to give reasons why this wasn't the best idea.

"No buts about it," Aunt Anna said firmly. "You can help *her* while *you* help me."

Fanny let out her breath, defeated. Now she needed to find a way out of this predicament. But how? She had two days to find a solution. Maybe Ollie could come up with something. She would spend the rest of the evening contemplating what she could say to change her aunt's mind.

❖━━━━━❖

Friday evening, after school is done for the day, Ollie has a plan she hopes she can pull off. Ollie knocks on the Smalls' door. She steps inside and tells Aunt Anna that her mother is very sick at home with a fever. "The only thing she hasn't been able to finish in the hems in the ten dresses. Surely, you would allow Fanny come over to our home and help out with the dresses. I'm not much of a seamstress, but

Fanny is great with the hems. If she doesn't get the dresses to the clothing store, she'll lose her commission for the month. It's really important for my mom, who wants to take you and Fanny out sometime for a nice lunch to show her appreciation. Please, Mrs. Small, couldn't you manage without Fanny for one day."

Olivia had a way of stating her case, making you think the world is on the verge of collapsing down around us if things aren't done in the way she lays out.

Aunt Anna stood listening as Olivia rambled on, and finally, just before the end, she starts sobbing uncontrollably.

"It's going be fine, then, Ollie. It's against my better judgment, but Fanny can go over to help your mother with the hems. Perhaps, in the future, your mother ought not to take on more consignments than she can manage without extra help." Anna patted the crying girl's shoulder.

Somehow, the ruse worked. The two girls just needed to keep Mrs. Reynolds out of sight in the event anyone came around on Saturday. They were pretty satisfied with all the devious stories they made up to get to do what they wanted; they wanted freedom from school, parents, aunts, and uncles and anyone else who tried to get in the way. Ollie came up with an ingenious scheme: she wrote a letter, disguising her handwriting, of course, and pretended to be her aunt, her mom's older sister who lived in Norfolk, West Virginia. She said she could really use her help right now because their father wasn't doing too well. Ollie knew that much to be true from the recent letter they had received from Ollie's grandma, lamenting her father's decline in the passing years. The real genius part of the letter was when she insisted Vera say nothing to their father about this letter. That way, they were covered on all sides.

The two girls slapped their hands together when the letter was posted, just in time for their second trip into Kingston. *My*, they both thought, *we are really clever*.

After the two girls had settled into Ollie's bed for the night, Fanny asked Ollie how she managed to come off so sincerely upset about the story she had concocted. "Well, this helped," Ollie explained as she held up a bottle of vodka. "It worked like a charm." She winked at Fanny, extending the bottle toward her to share it with her.

Fanny's eyes became large, and her mouth fell open, shocked, at what her friend was suggesting.

"Are you crazy?! I've never had anything alcoholic in my entire life! Aunt Anna said that even when she and Uncle George got married, they didn't serve it. I can't believe you! Where did you get it?" Fanny's mind whirled, trying to take in and digest the fact that Ollie drank alcohol.

"It's fine, don't be an old stick in the mud, Fanny. Besides, it makes you…forget all your troubles…and…makes you feel like…you can be anyone…and do…anything!" And with that being said, Ollie took a long drink from the bottle. "Come on…" She wiggled the bottle in front of

Fanny's face, like a carrot in front of a horse. "You know you want to…"

Fanny took the bottle but sat in on the bedside table, saying, "I'm not doing any such thing, Olivia Reynolds! I'm really surprised at you!" She attempted to sound like her Aunt Anna when she was being scolded.

"And you haven't told me where you got it," Fanny continued, looking stern.

"Someone I did a favor for," Olivia winked again, making Fanny wonder what manner of a "favor" Ollie was talking about.

"It's okay." Ollie shrugged her shoulders, pretending not to care one way or the other. "If you're scared, it's okay."

"I AM NOT scared," declared Fanny loudly. And as if to prove her point, she picked up the bottle and took a tentative sip. She coughed and felt as though her throat were on fire, continued coughing, but took another sip, this time getting a big swig down.

"There!" Fanny said, triumphantly. "I told you I wasn't scared."

"Good for you, little girl," Ollie said, "'cause you'll need it when I introduce you to my friend tomorrow," and Ollie turned over, as if to sleep.

"Wait a minute," Fanny tugged on Ollie's shoulder, "what friend?"

Ollie rolled back over on her back and said, "He's a sailor and just into Kingston Port for two days starting Saturday. He asked me to bring a friend for *his* friend, so…"

Fanny put both hands over her face. Both her eyes were wide as saucers as she replied, "I don't believe it! You set me up! How could you do that without even discussing it with me first?" Fanny felt elated and horrified all at the same time.

"Because you'd have said, 'no way,'" Ollie answered.

Quite correctly, Fanny thought. Fanny fell back against the pillows, not sure how to digest this last bit of information. It could be SO much fun! Or it could be disastrous. What if he takes one look at me and runs the other direction?

Fanny was lost in momentary thought, when Ollie's voice broke through her reverie, "Don't worry, Fan. These guys have been on a boat for six months. They'll think any girl is gorgeous."

Not convinced she wanted to be thought of as gorgeous for that reason, she calmly said, "Well, I haven't been on a boat for six months, and HE needs to meet MY qualifications!"

"I'm sure he will…," Ollie's voice drifted off, this time she really was falling asleep.

Fanny, however, her mind beginning to swirl from the vodka she drank, lay awake imagining the upcoming day and what might be in store.

13

A Day to Remember

When Fanny and Ollie arrived in Kingston that Saturday, the first place they headed for was the Lighthouse Diner. First thing after making the delivery of dresses for Ollie's mother, that is. The Diner, so named because it had been an old lighthouse converted into a diner. It was located, as lighthouses usually are, near the docks. The two waited expectantly, scanning the faces of each person who walked through the door of the diner.

Finally, two fellows decked out in sailor attire walked in. Ollie squealed, practically jumping over the table in a mad scramble to reach the first one. They both laughed as the sailor lifted Ollie off her feet and planted an uncomfortably long kiss on her lips. Fanny blushed and pretended to look out the diner window at the ships coming into port.

As they strolled back to the table arm in arm, Ollie introduced Fanny.

"Robert, this is my pal, Fanny Small. Fanny, Robert," Ollie was wearing her one-hundred-watt smile.

"And this," she continued, pulling him from behind Robert, "is Fred."

Fred allowed a smile to linger fleetingly over his face. As his head lowered, Robert punched him from behind.

He grabbed the sailor hat from his head as he extended his hand to Fanny. "Hi, I'm Fred," he repeated, pumping Fanny's proffered hand as though he was pumping water from a well.

"Hello, Fred, so nice to meet you." Fanny smiled somewhat nervously.

"Real nice weather for October, doncha think?" Fred commented as he sat down.

"Oh, shucks," Ollie laughed, "it's still summer here." She barely took her eyes off of Robert's face.

Ollie kept whispering in Robert's ear, and both Fred and Fanny looked very uncomfortable. Fanny was determined to come off with a winning personality, broached the subject of the navy by asking Fred, "How long have you served?"

Fred gave Fanny a nonplussed stare, and she continued, "You know, in the navy?"

"Oh, I see." he shook his head. "Six months now, this month."

Again, silence between them was loud while Robert and Ollie had eyes only for one another and played whispering games. Robert, not taking his eyes off of Ollie's face, said, "We're gonna get going now. You two have a swell day together."

And just like that, they were up and out the door. Fanny couldn't believe the turn of events. Just like she had manipulated Fanny into this blind date, now she was ditching her. To make matters worse, she ditched her with this fellow she didn't know at all.

"I...," Fanny stuttered out, "you don't have to stay with me. I don't expect you to..." She was both embarrassed and angry for being in this predicament. How could Ollie do this to her?

"No...I'd like to...if you don't mind, that is," Fred said, really looking at her, and Fanny looked back at him. He has nice eyes, she thought. She also thought he must think her lazy eye atrocious. If he did, he didn't mention it.

"Are you sure?" she questioned, secretly hoping he wouldn't change his mind.

"Sure," he said, smiling at her.

"All right, then," she said, glad that he wanted to stay with her. Otherwise, she would have had to find something to occupy her time until the boat could ferry her back across the Holden River.

"Are you hungry?" Fred asked, reaching for the menu.

"A little," Fanny replied, thinking she couldn't eat a bite. She was a bundle of nerves.

The couple ordered and ate amidst questions and answers to one another. From a distance, if anyone had been watching them, they might have thought them good friends. Each was genuinely interested in what the other had to say, and the air was punctuated with an occasional burst of laughter from one or both of them. Before they realized it, two hours had drifted by.

"So what do you think we should do now?" Fred asked.

"Well, Ollie and I visited the museum the last time we came, so…how about the zoo? I heard it's a really nice one," Fanny suggested hopefully.

"Great, I'd enjoy seeing my relatives today," Fred said very seriously.

"Relatives?" Fanny looked puzzled.

"You know…" Fred started to imitate chimpanzees, making a long face and arching his arms, scratching his sides.

"Ohhh…how funny!" Fanny laughed, and taking her by the arm, Fred escorted her out the door and to the Kingston zoo.

The day passed delightfully for Fanny. In fact, by the end of it, she fancied herself in love. Not so much with Fred, but with life in general. He was nice and courteous. All in all, Fred was a very likeable fellow. Somehow, he just didn't measure up to Ben Morris.

When she asked Fred for the time, she realized they had just enough time to return to the boat landing—if she ran all the way. She said, "Thank you for a lovely day," and without another word, Fanny began a frantic race toward the boat dock. Fred was left, looking rather bewildered, probably the way the prince looked when Cinderella had run away, leaving only a glass slipper. Unfortunately, Fred didn't even have that left to remember his day with Fanny Small.

Fanny reached the boat in just enough time to pay her fare and board. She did not see Ollie. She wasn't worried about her, though. She was still angry with her for the rotten way she had been used. She wouldn't have ever done something so despicable to her.

She sat, clinging to her hat, as the boat pulled away from the shore. Maybe Aunt Anna was right when she said Ollie was too independent. She remembered how Ollie hung all over Robert but felt a tug of jealousy just the same. *No man would ever act like that over me*, she thought to herself, *especially not Ben Morris*. Fanny was actually glad she was on her way home.

14

The Ups and Downs of Friendship

Since the ditching incident, Fanny decided to cool things with Ollie for a while. When she saw her at school, she ignored her. Undaunted by Fanny's cool treatment of her, Ollie formed other friendships, or so it seemed. Toward the end of the school year, with talk of graduation to come in the spring, Fanny found herself lonely for the friendship she had enjoyed with Ollie.

Fanny approached Ollie on the road home from school one day.

"Ollie," she called out to her as she was ahead of Fanny on the path.

Ollie turned around, and unsmiling, she said, "What?"

"I thought maybe we could get together sometime."

"Really?" Ollie's serious demeanor breaking into a smile.

"Yes, really," Fanny laughed as Ollie came racing into her arms, hugging her so hard Fanny thought she was breaking her ribs.

"But…," Fanny's tone became all business, "don't ever do something like that to me again!"

"Promise, I won't." Ollie held out her hand as a sign of truce.

"Okay then!" Fanny laughed as the girls continued to walk home.

◆————◆

Fanny and Ollie stayed out of Kingston, at least without permission from Aunt Anna for Fanny's part. Graduation came and went, and the two remained good friends.

Fanny's father continued to show up for the occasional dinner at the Small's home. To please her aunt, Fanny would attempt conversation with him, but it was stilted at best. Too many years of abandonment issues kept Fanny from feeling any kindness toward him. Memories of his late wife refused to let John Small cultivate a real relationship with his daughter. These dinner times usually ended with Fanny requesting an early dismissal from the table. Her father no longer made any objections.

Jimmy left home and married his longtime girlfriend, Sharon. They built a home close to the Small's. Aunt Anna loved Sharon; she knew she would be a good wife for her son. The marriage got Anna Small to thinking of fellows in Portage Bend who would be suitable for Fanny. She was now fourteen, prime age to bear and rear children while her body was strong and she still possessed unlimited energy.

When the subject was brought up, Fanny was flabbergasted and said so.

"Honestly, Aunt Anna, don't you think when I'm ready to get married, I can't find someone on my own?!" she said this rather loudly.

"Don't raise your voice to me, young lady," her aunt retorted. "Yes, I do think you can, but a little help never hurt anyone."

"That depends on what you consider helping," Fanny said, taking care to lower her voice.

"Well, we could have a Sunday barbecue after church one Sunday," Anna suggested, "and just sort of put the word out, you know…"

"What?! Oh, sure, make an announcement during church, why don't you?" raved Fanny. "If anyone would be interested in marrying Fanny Small, there's a free dinner in it for you!"

Fanny stomped off in a huff that day.

The years went by quicker than either her aunt or uncle or herself had the time to acknowledge their passing. It was only after the fact that they could marvel how it passed in what seemed like a moment.

Now she was seventeen, and Fanny was no closer to matrimony than the day Aunt Anna had brought up the subject. The final blow to Fanny's heart came when Ben Morris married a third cousin of his from Kingston. Maybe her aunt was right. She should have advertised for a beau when she was younger. Though only seventeen, Fanny felt much older. She prayed that God would not deprive her of children. That was her greatest wish: to mother a child.

15

Fulfillment of Duty

John Small had managed fairly well in spite of his diagnosis until the past month. He began to be troubled with a hacking cough that eventually drew blood. Each coughing episode brought on extreme fatigue, forcing him to rest for a sizeable amount of time. When he finally was left to lie in bed with barely the ability to turn over, he knew his death was close at hand.

Uncle George had been looking in on his brother regularly since he became ill. Now, it appeared John would be needing a full time caretaker.

Uncle George sat down with his wife and Fanny that evening to discuss what needed to be done.

"Fanny, I know the two of you have never been close, but he *is* your father. Remember, you wouldn't be here if not for him," Uncle George said this, his eyes looking directly into Fanny's.

"You have been more of a father to me than him," Fanny said.

"Perhaps, in one sense of the word. He needs help, and I'm afraid the burden is falling to you to carry out the need." Her uncle leaned forward, placing his hand on her face.

"Me?!" Fanny cried. "I can't...I won't...you can't expect me..." She faltered for words to make them understand.

"Sweetheart," Aunt Anna said softly, "it's your duty as a Christian woman to care for your father in his old age. I have been meaning to talk to you about this sooner, but I kept putting it off. Your uncle and I aren't getting any younger. We can't take care of the farm like it needs to run properly. We sold the place..."

"What?!" Fanny was aghast at the news. "I can't believe you're selling the farm. I grew up here. I can't leave it." Fanny started to cry as her aunt continued.

"Yes, it's true. We've sold it, and both of us are moving in with Jimmy and Sharon. They are moving to Jonestown to be near Sharon's family, and we're going with them. I'm sorry, Fanny."

"Fanny, it seemed the sensible thing for us to do," Uncle George said. "Your father needs you, so it all is going to work out."

"Please don't make me go!" she pleaded, grabbing her aunt's hands in her own. "I'll die if I have to go there, I'll just die!"

"It's the way things are meant to be," her aunt said, patting Fanny's hands as she gripped them in her own.

John Small's house was not large. He originally planned to add on as the family increased in number. Since that had never been a possibility, the house had stayed as it had started. It consisted of one large room with a fireplace on one wall, a counter with a pump on another, and a bed pushed up in one corner. After the death of Bessy Small, John had found little use for making repairs, and the fifteen years of neglect were evident. Fanny used a small spot near the fireplace to make a bed where she could sleep. She used a blanket to cushion the wooden floor beneath her.

Her father had little to say upon her arrival. The illness had sapped his strength so that he was bedridden. The worst part of taking care of him was placing the bedpan beneath his bottom so that he could relieve himself. And then, removing it and cleaning it. Fanny wanted to gag, and frequently did, performing this odious task. The job of caregiving to someone one loved would be a hard task, at best. Doing this manner of care to one you openly have disgust for is unbearable.

He abused her verbally on a daily basis. She tried to shave her father with the straight razor the first morning. The day she approached him with utensils ready to proceed, he said, "What do you think you're gonna do with those?" he demanded.

"Your whiskers need taken off," she replied.

"Go to hell," he spat out at her. He used other expletives too vile to put on paper.

He turned in his bed so his backside faced her. Good enough, Fanny thought to herself, she may very well have sliced his neck open in the process. She never approached him again to attempt to shave his face.

A week into her stay in her father's house, he was feeling well enough to sit up in bed. Fanny was busy washing the breakfast dishes. He watched her as she did so, and he asked her a question she did not expect.

"Why did you come here?" his tone of voice was gruff with suspicion.

"I came," she said softly, "to take care of you during your last days."

"But why?" he asked again.

"Because…it is the Christian thing to do."

"You think you're a Christian? My wife is dead because of you! You are no better than a whore walking the streets of Kingston." His eyes blazed with hatred toward Fanny.

She felt as though she had been punched in the stomach, hard. Tears sprang to her eyes she fiercely fought to keep them back, and she responded, "I didn't…I didn't do it on purpose. Do you think I didn't want to have a mother? I was robbed of a mother and a father. You have not been a father to me, not even a little bit! Haven't I suffered enough?"

"Suffer?" he said softly. "You don't know what suffering is. I lost the one person I loved more than anything or anyone in this world. Because of YOU!"

Fanny's hands covered her face, and the tears could be held back no longer. She ran to the valise that held her belongings, slamming it shut. She lifted it and said as she walked out the front door, "I can't stay here any longer. If staying here is the Christian thing to do…well, then, I can't be a Christian any longer."

She left the Small house, not knowing where she should go. She walked to the barn, and there she worked out a plan in her mind. She wouldn't go back to her aunt and uncle's home—they would only force her to come back here. She had a little money Aunt Anna had given her when she left, and Fanny had found a gold broach her first time cleaning at her father's home. She assumed it had belonged to her mother. Without asking, Fanny had hidden it in her valise beneath all her clothing. She guessed that made her a thief as well as denouncing her religion as she forsook her father. It seemed fitting under the circumstances.

Fanny made up her mind to take the boat across the Holden River to Kingston. From there, she would see how far the money she had would take her. Beyond that, she would have to wait and see.

16

Decisions

Fanny awoke. At first, she didn't know where she was, but then she remembered. She had walked out on her father—her sick and dying father. The straw she had slept on stuck onto her face as she sat upright. She swept it aside, wondering what she should do now. One fact she knew for sure, she was not going back into that house. He could lay there until he was dead for all she cared. Her once-tender and loving spirit had been replaced with a cold stone that seemed to sit heavily in her chest.

How had all this happened and so quickly? Why, only a few days ago, she was happy. At least, as happy as she had ever been. She stood, smoothing out her dress the best she could. Her mouth felt as though she had swallowed cotton. She picked up her small suitcase and walked out of the barn. As she walked to the pump to draw a drink of water, she was amazed that the sun was still bright and the sky an azure blue. The leaves of the trees were ready to bloom. In another month, they would. It seemed at odds with how she felt inside. Didn't the sun know she was miserable? Didn't the sky realize she needed it to reflect how she felt?

She used to pray in situations such as this. But no prayer could form on her lips. Surely Jesus had forsaken her just as surely as she had rejected him. She had no one, only herself.

She walked down the path until she reached the Reynolds's home. She knocked on their door, not knowing what she would say to either Mrs. Reynolds or to Ollie. Ollie answered the knock, with a small boy on her hip. The child was about a year old, a product of Ollie's free and easy lifestyle.

"Good morning, Ollie," Fanny said. She couldn't bring herself to even smile. The little boy looked at Fanny and quickly hid his face in his mother's shoulder.

"Fanny, are you all right?" Ollie asked with concern. "I thought you'd be with your father."

"I am…I mean…I was, but now, I'm not." She wondered what Ollie would think of her, leaving her father in his time of need.

"Come on in, Fan." Ollie stepped aside to invite her into the house. "What's going on?"

"I left. That's what is going on." Fanny said simply. Once she said it, it sounded normal, not something horrible or evil.

"Left…your father?" Ollie's face showed she didn't understand what a powerful statement Fanny had just made.

"Yes. I left him. He hates me. He has always hated me, and he blames me for my mother's death. I couldn't stay there another minute." Fanny said all this without tears, and she realized that she felt surprisingly little emotion.

"Oh no, Fanny," Ollie said, putting her son down. His pajama clad feet promptly took off. "I know the two of you were never really close, but he doesn't *hate* you, I'm sure."

"Yes, he does. He told me so," Fanny said, looking downward, somehow embarrassed by the fact that her own father didn't love her.

"Oh." Ollie was, for once, at a loss for words.

"I thought...I mean...I was hoping...your mother wouldn't mind too much if I cleaned up a bit. I slept in the barn on his property. I must look like it too."

"Of course, of course you can. She'd insist on it. Just use the basin in my room. Are you hungry?"

"No...well, maybe later. I just need to clean up."

"Sure." Ollie placed a hand on Fanny's shoulder and guided her to the bedroom the two of them had slept in so many times, talking and laughing about girlish things. Those times seemed like a life time ago.

Once freshened, Fanny felt like she could think clearly again. She made up her mind to travel somewhere new, where folks couldn't judge her, and start her life over. She wasn't sure where she wanted to go. She would decide when she got to the train station in Kingston. Upon telling her plans to Ollie, her friend just looked at Fanny as though she thought she was a bit crazy.

"Fanny, you've always been the one who was scared to try anything. You have always been so good, never breaking the rules. I had to talk you into everything we did, and now you are going, *by yourself*! And you don't even know where and attempt to start over? Who are you, and what did you do with my friend, Fanny?"

"Look, I know I was never very daring. It's true. But I have no home here anymore. You know my aunt and uncle moved away with Jimmy and his wife. I can't stay and take care of that vile man. I have to do this." Fanny's voice was firm, her shoulders held back with a look of determination that convinced herself and Ollie she could do what she said she was going to do.

"You can stay here, you know. With me and Mama and Robert," Ollie said.

"That's really nice of you," Fanny said, with complete sincerity, "I really appreciate it, but no, this is what I have to do."

Ollie nodded, staring at Fanny's face, and said, "All right. I'll go with you to the train station."

◆———◆

After an hour of walking around the train depot, Fanny insisted Ollie leave her there.

"I'll write you when I get to wherever I decide to go," assured Fanny

"Are you sure you'll be all right by yourself? I can stay…" Ollie said with concern.

"Yes! Just go. I need to think, make a decision."

"All right." Ollie gave her one last hug and then left Fanny sitting on a bench in the Kingston Rail Station.

Aunt Anna and Uncle George had given her one-fourth of the sale of the farm. It really didn't amount to much when you were on your own, but it would help get her started. She studied the arrivals and departure grid over and over and at last decided Chicago would be her new home. She bought a one-way ticket and boarded the first train heading for the windy city.

One last look at Kingston and surrounding countryside and then the train was taking her to a new city and a new life. Only God knew what was ahead of her, she thought. He did know, and He was with her even though she didn't know it.

17

Chicago

As the train sped along its route heading toward Chicago, Fanny settled back for the ride.

Fanny wondered how long it would take for word to get to Aunt Anna and Uncle George in Jonestown that she had abandoned her father. Well, if they really had cared about her, they wouldn't have forced her to go there to take care of a man who hated the very sight of her. The anger she felt toward her aunt and uncle surprised her. She realized she'd never felt any negative emotion toward them before. She was a little unsettled by it.

For right now, she would enjoy the novelty of the train trip. A new experience, hopefully, one of many yet to come. She observed the rolling hills dotted with cattle and bails of alfalfa. When she tired of scenery, she looked about the train car at the other people. A gentleman in a bowler hat and suit sat engrossed in his daily paper. A large woman wearing a ruffled bonnet held a sleeping child. She smiled at Fanny when their eyes met. A small fellow impatiently tapping his feet on the metal floor gazed at the train car ceiling.

The ticket taker had said it would be an eight-hour trip to Chicago. She decided to nap in order to pass the time more quickly. She rested her head against the window, closing her eyes. Her mind would not stop working, however. It kept reliving the last horrible minutes with her father. The painful words spoken, the feeling of pain and suffocation, and the urgent need to escape those surroundings. What would Uncle George and Aunt Anna be thinking of her when they learned of her actions? The initial anger having subsided; anxiety was setting in uncomfortably in its place. She sighed, wishing the thoughts away. After several hours of relentless mental anguish, her body no longer fought sleep. She slept as though exhausted.

When she awoke, it was daylight. The sun shone brightly and glistened off the metallic exterior of the train. She whispered to the woman with the child, who was now awake and was climbing all over his mother, "Do you know where we are?"

"Just south of Chicago, another hour or so," the woman replied as she fought to keep the child seated on her lap.

Fanny thanked her for the information and readied herself for the arrival in the big city of Chicago.

Fanny exited the train car behind the other travelers. She was in awe at the mere size of the Chicago train depot. The ceilings alone stretched upward of twelve feet or more. The depot seemed to be endless, with wall-to-wall people as far as her eye could see. A bench nearby beckoned. Perhaps she should sit here and think about what to do next. She was hoping to find a place that would allow her to clean or cook in exchange for a place to stay. That would only be temporary until she could arrange something on a permanent basis.

Within a few moments of having sat down, a man came and sat on the bench next to her. He wasn't really young but didn't appear what one would say was old. He said good morning and inquired if this was her first time to the city. She said yes. She quietly studied this fellow out of the corner of her eye when he was looking in the opposite direction. They sat on the bench together for some time in silence, and glancing at his pocket watch, he seemed about to vacate his seat there. She took a chance and trying her best to sound like an adult, she asked him, "Sir, do you know of a good place to spend the night that is clean and safe?" He was a good-looking fellow Fanny couldn't help but notice. He said he was a businessman and knew of a lady she could stay with, and she might even have a job for her, if, that is, she was interested. What kind of business was he in, Fanny inquired. Was it a hotel or a restaurant, something of that nature? She was pretty sure she could handle a job cooking or cleaning, so it was with a hopeful heart that she asked that question.

He said it was a service-oriented business, and the lady was the manager. Fanny could scarcely believe how fortunate she had been to have sat down and met someone who could guide her to a place to stay and a job. This is exactly what she had hoped. While she thanked him profusely, he smiled and said it was his pleasure to be of service. He even offered to take her there himself.

Innocent as she was to the ways of the world, Fanny readily accepted his offer. He told her his name was Joel Patterson and described his business as one that satisfied the needs of a "high class" clientele. He delivered services that couldn't be found at any other venue. Fanny's curiosity was definitely piqued, and she envisioned a fine-looking establishment with cut crystal chandeliers and plush carpeting. She'd read about hotels such as these in *The Ladies' Home Journal*.

"Really!" she gushed, somewhat like the schoolgirl she recently had been. He nodded and chuckled at Fanny's wide-eyed amazement of everything he told her. He said he had an appointment to keep, so if she wanted him to accompany her to the business, they needed to leave immediately.

Fanny was oblivious to the fact that Joel Patterson used the Chicago train depot to scope out girls and women; anyone that appeared vulnerable or desperate. He *was*, in fact, a businessman. He had not told Fanny any lies;

he just allowed her to perceive what he said in her own innocent way. If she could only have known that he had an entire map of train depots, roadside rest areas, even schools that he used as his hiring ground. Some of the girls were runaways, like Fanny. Others were seeking an escape from abusive homes, still others were just adventure seekers.

She relished seeing all the skyscrapers and window dressings of all the fine stores the two of them passed after exiting the train depot. It was all a little dreamlike to her; only in her wildest thoughts did she ever imagine she would be here, seeing these sights. She told herself, someday, she would have lots of money and she would shop in these impressive-looking stores. She would have a nice home in a nice area of town.

Patterson hailed a cab and gave the address to the driver. Upon hearing it, the cabbie took a long look at Fanny and asked her how old she was. She squirmed inwardly at his gaze and Fanny replied that she was almost seventeen, trying to stand straight to her full five-foot three-inch height.

"Pickin' 'em a little young, ain'tcha?" he asked Patterson quizzically.

"Just take us to the address, cabbie," he answered in a clipped tone that kept the driver from asking any more questions.

Fanny wondered what difference her age made anyway. Back in Porter's Bend, girls of the same age and younger were already married and had borne two or three children.

She would certainly be able to handle some cooking and cleaning.

As the cab moved through the city streets, she took it all in. She wondered if had she not been running away, would she ever have gotten to see such wonderful things? Probably not, she mused. She didn't think Uncle George or Aunt Anna had been any place beyond the Kingston city limits. Well, she was here now, and she would savor the experience.

She couldn't help but notice the scenery was changing from the posh-looking storefronts to buildings that appeared older. She observed refuse on the curbs, pushed there by the force of the wind. Some men were huddled over a trash can that a fire was set in, warming their hands. The men looked somewhat disheveled and their clothing tattered. Well, she thought, this is no neighborhood for a classy hotel or restaurant. So it was with trepidation she asked Joel, "Your business isn't right around here, is it?"

"Relax. The inside is much nicer than it looks on the outside. We have to keep things discreet, so not to attract attention," he explained, although Fanny didn't understand what he meant at all. Seems to me he'd want to attract customers, she thought.

The cab pulled up to a red brick building; there were no windows, only a single door. Patterson paid the fare and helped Fanny out of the cab. The wind was brisk. Her hair blew around her face with the force of it. She shivered with the cold. It had been so much warmer in Tennessee, she thought to herself. She had only a thin winter coat, and that was back in a closet at her aunt and uncle's home. The winters were always so mild there a heavy coat wasn't needed. She could see that wasn't going to be the case here.

She felt a slight bit of apprehension as she gazed around at the surroundings. Had she made a mistake trusting a stranger? Well, it was too late to change her mind now. He led her through the door of the building. They traveled up a staircase that led down a long hallway. Patterson knocked a rat-a-tat-tat with his knuckles on one of the doors. It was apparent he was signaling to someone inside that it was him.

The door swung open. Framed in the shadowy light emanating from within was a woman with the largest bosom Fanny had ever seen. The woman was dressed in less than a modest fashion. The dress she wore was beautiful, Fanny thought, but so low cut! She blushed, just standing there while she was introduced to Lulu, who, according to Joel, was the head of the operation. Lulu's hair was piled up high atop her head and her eyes and lips looked like nothing Fanny had ever seen before. But when she smiled, she seemed genuinely nice. A gold tooth glinted out of her mouth at Fanny.

"Come on in, honey," Lulu sounded enthusiastic.

Maybe it wasn't as bad as she thought. As they proceeded into the room, Fanny was amazed at all the girls, sitting on sofas and chairs. All of them looked like thinner versions of Lulu; some were young, some not so young. A few of them were smoking. One of them hooted upon seeing Fanny alongside Joel.

"Hah! Gotcha a new baby," one of the older women said and laughed loudly.

"Oooh, Joel! Is she any good?" another oozed in a sultry tone.

"Be quiet, Annabelle," Joel said, in a tone that suggested she had better stop kidding around. Fanny wondered what the comments were supposed to mean; she suddenly wished she was more sophisticated and knowledgeable. It was downright embarrassing. She felt shaky inside, and she fiddled with her hair with her free hand out of sheer nervousness. She carried the valise in her other hand.

"Lulu here, she'll take care of you. Just do what she tells you and you'll be fine," Joel talked with his head near Fanny's ear and then turned as if to go.

Fanny was alarmed at the prospect of being left here with all these…ladies.

"You're not going, are you? I mean…you're not going to leave me here alone, are you?"

"Don't worry," Joel said, trying to use a soothing tone of voice.

"Lulu will take good care of you, I promise!" And with that, he turned and walked out the same door he had brought her through. The women lounging about had lost interest in her as fast as Joel walked out. There was one girl. She didn't look much older than Fanny. She was the only one who actually smiled as she and Fanny exchanged glances.

Fanny just stood there, looking at the unfamiliar surroundings. All the windows had newspaper over them, blocking out any scenery. Although, from what she had seen on her way in, the newspaper was probably better scenery than what was outside those windows. It was a large room that had been cordoned off with curtains. Over the top of each curtain, there was a different colored scarf. They looked like a transparent-type material, each one draped in a unique fashion. All the girls wore clothing unlike anything Fanny had ever seen. Aunt Anna would never have sewn together anything like any of these!

"Hungry, honey?" Lulu asked, and she put her rather hefty arm around Fanny's slim shoulders.

"Yes...I am, a little," Fanny answered softly. "I didn't have a chance to eat anything after I got off the train."

"Right off the train, huh?" Lulu said, shaking her head. Fanny didn't know why she said that or why she was shaking her head.

"Is this where all the maids for the hotel stay?" Fanny inquired as Lulu guided her into a smaller room with a table and chairs. There was a small icebox there as well. Lulu opened the icebox door and pulled out a ham and a slab of cheese. She pulled out a loaf of bread from the cupboard.

As she assembled a sandwich, she asked Fanny, "Hotel? Is that what Patterson told you?"

"Yes…I mean, no…not exactly. I guess…I just assumed he owned a hotel…or maybe a restaurant. See, I asked him if he knew of a place where I could cook or clean in exchange for a place to sleep. What sort of business is this?" Fanny asked, her voice a little shaky with the fit of nerves she was experiencing.

"Well…," Lulu started to explain to her, "we provide *services* to men." She handed Fanny the sandwich and reached into the icebox and pulled out a quart of milk. She poured a glass of it and placed it in front of her.

"Do you get what I'm saying?" Lulu's eyebrows rose as she asked the question.

Fanny was so hungry she started eating the food and drank down the milk in large gulps in between bites.

"No, I don't," she said as she ate. "I'm sorry. I guess I'm not very smart about how things are done outside Porter's Bend."

"Porter's what? Never mind that. Do you even *know* about sex?" Lulu sat opposite Fanny with her large arms crossed on the table in front of her.

Once again, Lulu was shaking her head.

Fanny was somewhat shocked at hearing that word. No one ever used that word back home. They would use some kind of code word for it, like, "wifely duty," but never the actual word. Well, it made sense, considering how Lulu and the others were dressed. It was something she and Ollie would whisper about when the two spent the night together, back when they were still schoolgirls. Before Ollie ended up pregnant. Obviously, Ollie knew much more about sex than Fanny did.

"Well…I know what it *is*, if that's what you mean."

"Well, I guess it's fallen to me to educate you," Lulu said matter-of-factly.

Then Lulu began to talk. Occasionally, she'd ask Fanny if she had any questions. Stupefied, Fanny realized she had been manipulated into coming to a brothel, a whorehouse, as she had heard boys from school days call such a place.

"And who are the customers?" she asked, not quite knowing what she was supposed to say at this point.

"Oh, men who are lonely. Some of them have wives who can't or won't, and there are men who think it makes them more of a man." Lulu said all this like she had encountered them all and as though it was perfectly normal to have a vocation like this.

"Lulu, I don't think I can work here. I don't think it's right. No offense to you…," she added hastily.

"Okay, no problem," she said, "but you're gonna find out the streets of Chicago is not a place for a little girl like you." Lulu locked eyes with Fanny. "You know," continued Lulu, "I'm not like a lot of madams in this city. I keep a safe place for my girls to stay. They get three square meals a day, and we do a fifty-fifty split. If a guy gets rough, I call the police. No one mistreats one of *my* girls."

"The police?" Fanny said naively. "But isn't...doing what you do...illegal?"

"Well," Lulu said, with a glint in her eyes, "I take care of a couple of them, and they return the favor, if you get what I mean."

Fanny sat, mulling over the situation. If she left here, she had no place else to go. Who knew what she could run into on these city streets? She remembered scriptures from her little white Bible about sexual immorality being a sin. Hphm. If God had been there for her, she would not be in this predicament in the first place. She was the one now shaking her head. She also remembered that she hadn't picked up her Bible when she left her father's house in such a rush.

"I've never...I don't know anything..." Fanny faltered for the proper words. The idea of doing what Lulu had described to her left her feeling both intrigued and sickened, all at the same time. How had she gotten herself into this mess? It seemed as though God wasn't looking out for her anymore, she thought sadly. Then she felt anger toward God again. He had allowed all this to happen to her; being forced to go to her father's, hearing him tell her he hated her and blamed her for something she had no control over. What did His word matter now?

She took a deep breath and said, "All right. I'll do it."

18

Dressing for the Part

Lulu set about getting Fanny prepared to go to work. The first order of business was sending her to an eye doctor. He fitted her up with a pair of glasses made for the purpose of strengthening the muscle in the lazy eye. Fanny was so excited at the prospect of having normal-looking eyes she kept hugging Lulu, and then she would look into the mirror, turning her head this way and that to see how she looked in the glasses. The doctor said it might take as long as a year to get the muscle strong enough. A year out of a lifetime was nothing, Fanny thought happily.

After the doctor, Lulu took her back to the house. There, she assigned Rose to teach Fanny how to dress, how to apply makeup, and of course, how to please a man. Rose took her into another room, which had been made into a huge closet. Fanny had never seen so many beautiful dresses or high-heeled shoes before in one place.

"Whose are all these?" she asked in wonderment, pulling out a sequined gown and examining it with awe.

"Lulu's. But all of us wear them." Rose watched Fanny as she held the dress, noting the way she looked: like a starry eyed child at Christmas time.

Rose was a stunning woman with a statuesque figure. She had flaming red hair swept up on one side and held with rhinestone hair clip. She had on heavy makeup, but it was flawless. She told Fanny she had been in the business for ten years. Fanny thought she had never seen a woman as beautiful as Rose.

"You can wear that"—she motioned to the dress she held in her hands—"if you want."

"Really?" Fanny had never had anything remotely like that dress. "All right, I'd love to wear it!"

With the dress on, Fanny realized, as she gazed in the full-length mirror, that she actually had a nice figure. No one could ever have known that wearing the shapeless dresses and aprons of back home, she thought. The high heels were something else. How did anyone walk in these things, she asked Rose.

Rose showed her how to walk without falling down; she minced her steps, and Fanny followed suit, pleased how quickly she was able to master the technique.

Next, Rose sat Fanny down and did her makeup. When Rose was finished with her face, she twirled her around to face the mirror, saying, "Ta-da!" Fanny was mesmerized by her own face; why, she *almost* thought she looked pretty.

"Rose," Fanny's face lost the smiling delighted look and took on a seriously worried one as she asked, "I don't know how to…I'm not…How do I…" the full realization that it was not just a game of dress up. It was all to prepare her toward one end. She shook, sitting there, not knowing what to do.

"Relax. Let them do all the work. You are just along for the ride." Rose laughed and said, "You'll be fine, I promise."

She taught her to get the money in advance of rendering any services. And to hide the money until it was safely in Lulu's hands. Thievery among the women was rampant. She learned that Lulu had connections with powerful people so that there was nothing she couldn't provide for her girls.

19

Consequences

Rose introduced Fanny to all the other girls. They ranged in ages from fourteen to fifty-nine. Fanny was the newest member of the group. Lulu was the oldest. Fanny learned that the scarf-like material over each curtained off section was used to show who was working what section. This way Lulu was able to keep track of who worked and when, in the event someone decided to cheat her. Or at least try.

There were fifteen of them; Fanny added to the total, making it sixteen. Their names were as varied as their personalities; Rose, of course, and Delia, Annabelle, Liselle, Roberta, Claudia, Peg, Vanessa, Norma, Wilma, Caroline, Jeanie, Lou, Nicole, and Sarah.

Sarah was the young girl who had smiled at Fanny when she first arrived. She was only fourteen. Fanny told Rose it would take her awhile to remember all the names. She learned that working hours were from 6:00 p.m. until midnight, six nights a week. Sundays, no one worked. Fanny couldn't help but see the irony of that.

It turned out Lulu had the entire second floor of the building for use of the business. Some of the rooms were where the girls slept. They doubled up since the rooms were large. Fanny was placed with Rose because she had been number fifteen and had a room all to herself. Lulu had her own space as well. Lulu did not "work." She only kept the door during business hours, making sure only those who had been "cleared" or were sent by Patterson were allowed in.

They had a series of regular customers. A few of these had their preferred girl. If you were fortunate enough to land a regular, the cost was more, so you earned more. Fanny didn't understand why this was so, inquiring to Rose.

"Well, if they like one girl better than another, you know they'll pay more to have what they want," Rose told her simply.

"So you're taking advantage of them…," Fanny said, half jokingly.

"Honey, the taking advantage thing goes both ways." Rose smiled when she said this.

Seven of them worked at the same time, the next group of seven would work next. The odd number would substitute for each of the girls to give each girl another day off besides Sunday. It certainly seemed to be run efficiently, Fanny thought.

Fanny was scared and anxious at first, but that passed soon enough. She began to feel something she'd never felt before: confidence. And what's more, she felt pretty for the first time in her life. Aside from a small prickling of her conscience, she felt good. It was only when she lay down to sleep at night that troubling thoughts came to her. She remembered her father's words when he said she killed her mother. Did God think of her that way as well? Well, if she was going to be accused of being evil, she might as well actually be evil.

Each girl was paid on Saturday each week. The first pay astounded Fanny. She had not ever held so much cash in her own hands before. Rose took her aside that day and told her again the importance of hiding her money. Not everyone there was honest. She also told her not to fall for any sob stories. Some of these women think because you're young, you can be easily taken advantage of. Don't let them fool you that way.

She struck up something of a friendship with Sarah. She told Fanny that she started the same way she had. Patterson spotted her at the train depot, wandering around, begging for spare change. Sarah said she had left home because her father beat her. She had two other sisters, but she was the only one her father beat. She didn't know why. Sarah's voice trembled as she told Fanny her story. Fanny felt so sorry for her.

Sarah gave Fanny some advice.

"Don't keep this up. If you want a chance to have a decent life, get out as fast as you can. Sarah told her several of the girls had wanted to escape the brothel life. When others found out where they came from…they just ended up coming back here again. They always do." Sarah had a sound of helplessness and hopelessness as she spoke.

"And," she whispered, "whatever you do, don't fall in love. I did, and Lulu had him killed." Sarah turned her head away, but Fanny saw her tears.

"How did she kill him?" Fanny wanted to know.

"Lulu knows people. He walked out of his house one day and someone shot him in the head. He was going to get me out of here, and she knew it. And just like that, it was all over."

"She can't do that," Fanny said, in a horrified tone. "It's illegal, for one thing. And it's murder!"

Sarah shrugged her shoulders.

"Lulu can do anything she wants." She turned and left Fanny sitting on the edge of her bed, her mind reeling with the information she had just received. Rose had explained to Fanny about Lulu "knowing" people, but she could never have imagined she'd go so far as to kill someone she thought threatened her business. She looked around the room and thought none of this was in her plans when she left home. Maybe that was the problem. She had not had a plan, and she fell easily into Joel Patterson's scheme. She began to see Lulu for what she really was as well. A coldhearted businesswoman. Fanny, feeling so confident at first, now felt scared and panicky. She just had to be very, very careful.

Fanny did come up with a plan. She would save all the money she could and then she would leave the brothel. She had learned her way around Chicago pretty well by now. She missed her aunt and uncle, but she didn't think she could ever face either one of them again. She was sure Aunt Anna would know just by looking at her what she had done. It might as well be written across her forehead: whore. But what choice had she been left with? As with every time these kinds of thoughts beset her, Fanny justified her actions to herself. Guilt had become her constant companion. After a while, she was used to feeling that way.

After two months of working at the brothel, Fanny woke up one morning sick to her stomach. She raced to the bathroom she shared with Rose, making it in the nick of time. She heaved into the toilet. Maybe she ate something bad, she thought. If she didn't start feeling better, she would ask Lulu to allow this to be her day off. She lay back down across her bed, thinking another hour of sleep might help.

Rose came into the room, and seeing Fanny still in bed, she said, "Better get up. Lulu wants you and me to clean the kitchen. It's our turn, you know."

"Rose…could I…would you…"

"Look, we all have to take a turn," Rose said, hands on hips, thinking Fanny was trying to get out of her share of chores.

"No…it's not that…I'm sick…," moaned Fanny.

"Yeah, sure," Rose said, rolling her eyes. "I'm 'sick' too. Get up!"

Fanny rolled over, facing Rose. Rose noticed how red her face was and walked over, placing her hand on Fanny's forehead.

"Crap. I guess I have to clean up by myself," Rose said with resignation.

"Sorry, Rose," Fanny mumbled and pulled herself out of bed as another wave of nausea overwhelmed her. She ran to the toilet and heaved again.

"How long you been sick?" Rose asked.

"Just this morning. I think that tuna I ate yesterday was too old." Fanny gasped, sitting on her knees in the bathroom in front of the toilet.

"Well, I certainly hope it's not you know what." Rose idled toward the door.

Fanny did not reply. She didn't want to arouse any more suspicion. Fanny had missed her last period, but she thought it was just late. Now, she worried that Rose was right. She was you know what.

20

A Problem or a Blessing?

Lulu allowed Fanny to take the day off. She went straight to the doctor Lulu used for all the girls when one of them fell ill. She had made the excuse that she thought a little fresh air would make her feel better. She had no appointment but begged to be seen, so the doctor told her if she didn't mind waiting, he would see her. She knew she was taking a risk seeing him because he might tip off Lulu. If she were actually pregnant, she shuddered to think what Lulu's reaction would be. If she had not hesitated to kill a man to keep one of the girls in the business, it would scarcely cause her to blink to abort a child.

The doctor confirmed Fanny's fears. She was indeed with child. She took a chance and asked him not to inform Lulu she had come in and please, please not say anything about the pregnancy. Her eyes scanned the young doctor's face looking for some trace of compassion. He said he would not reveal the visit or her secret to anyone. Fanny kept thanking him over and over as she left his office.

Fanny didn't trust anyone right now who was involved in the business. Rose already suspected. The only one who she could confide in was Sarah. As soon as she got back to the brothel, Fanny sought Sarah out. The only place where they could have a private conversation was in the bathroom. Fanny stuffed a towel under the crack at the bottom of the door and a wad of toilet paper in the keyhole to muffle any eavesdropping.

She told Sarah she had just learned she was pregnant. She wasn't sure how to proceed. She didn't know anyone in the city who wasn't one of Lulu's lapdogs or a paying customer.

Sarah thought, and then she said, "I'll write down my mother's name and address. She doesn't know I'm living here, and she doesn't know what I'm doing. You have to promise you won't tell her either. Just tell her that I'm okay and that I said she would help you. And tell…her…that I love her." This last phrase was spoken so low that Fanny barely heard it.

"Do you think she will?" Fanny queried, unsure of anything at the moment.

"Yes, she will. She will, especially, if you tell her that you and I are friends."

"Oh, thank you so much, Sarah. I won't forget you for this. Why don't we both go? I know your mother would want you to come back home," Fanny pleaded with her.

"No, I can't," Sarah said, hanging her head down. "If my father is still alive, it will be just like it was before I ran away, and I can't go back to that."

"Listen, Sarah," Fanny continued, "if he's not there, I'll get word to you and you can go home, all right?"

"Sure." Sarah answered, but she did not look as if she held out any hope for that.

"You should leave tonight, when Lulu goes to bed for the evening. Just make sure she's asleep and go."

"What about Rose? She might wake up and get Lulu," fretted Fanny.

"I'll pretend I had a nightmare and come and get her," Sarah said this as though this had happened before at some point.

"That's a good plan," Fanny said, figuring Sarah knew what she was doing.

The plan was set, now all she needed to do was fulfill it.

21

A Place for Fanny

Just as they had planned earlier, Sarah knocked on Fanny and Rose's bedroom door around 2:15 that morning. She appeared to be crying, and she knelt by Rose's bedside. Rose awoke. Sarah was whispering something to her, all the while Fanny pretended to be asleep.

Rose got out of her bed and followed Sarah out of the room. Immediately, Fanny rose. She pulled her satchel from under the bed. She carried it with her to the door and peered into the hallway. She had gone to bed fully dressed, carefully pulling the bed covers up to her neck to avoid detection by Rose.

She saw no one in the corridor. Fanny tiptoed as quietly as she could, made her way to the stairs and out the front door. The shock of the cool night air hit her, causing her to awaken fully. Perhaps she should just find a doorway to stay in until daylight. She didn't think Sarah's mother would trust someone knocking on her door in the wee hours of a June morning.

Still, Fanny felt she needed to get far enough away in the event Rose returned to their room and alerted Lulu soon. If only she could disguise herself somehow. She pushed her hair back behind her ear, trying to think. It hit her, then. Her hair! She would cut it off. That would help since Lulu would certainly have her goons searching for a girl with long, brown hair. She quickened her step, crossing the street. She came to a trolley stop she was familiar with. She would wait only a few minutes to see if the trolley would come this way. If it did not, she would keep on walking.

Within two minutes, the bell of the trolley sounded, and she boarded the train with relief. Sarah's mother's address was on the other side of the city, a middle class neighborhood. She would get as close as she could and look for a place to wait and possibly get a bit of sleep while she waited for the daylight. The trolley was going to the next stop, about five miles away from her destination. When she arrived at the stop, she was gratified to see it was an actual trolley station. She went in; the place was deserted except for a sleepy eyed ticket taker.

Fanny saw a public restroom sign and she headed for that. There, in a stall she locked, she sat on a closed toilet, resting her feet on top of her suitcase. It wasn't very comfortable, so she opened her case, withdrawing a flannel gown. She rolled it into an oblong shape and used it for a pillow against her back. She could lean without discomfort now against the toilet's tank. She closed her eyes, but visions of an infuriated Lulu were all she could think about. She might even consider killing *her*, she thought in fear.

She tried to shake these thoughts, but they persisted. Well, Fanny realized, sleep was not going to be an option. She would just have to wait for the sun to come up.

She stayed in the toilet, hiding out for what seemed like forever. She ventured a peek out of the restroom. A few travelers were sitting, waiting for the next trolley. The sky's color was a milky gray, just predawn. If she got started now, it would probably be sunrise by the time she arrived at Sarah's home. Sarah's last name was Anderson. Her plan was to greet the woman of the house with, "Hello, Mrs. Anderson. I'm a friend of your daughter, Sarah. She sent me." She rehearsed the first conversation over and over in her head as she walked the five miles there. All the homes in this area were built in the late 1800s, so all them were less than fifty years old. The houses were all large, no doubt because the majority of home owners were Catholic.

Finally, her feet aching, she stood in front of a red brick porch attached to a white house with black shutters on the windows. She could tell the shutters were only for decoration. That was a sign of an upscale home. She approached the front door.

She saw a doorbell and used it. She waited. She rang again. And waited. What if they aren't here? What if they had moved for some reason? But then she heard the sound of someone's footsteps within the house. She stood up straighter, preparing her speech.

The door opened, and a child stood there, wide eyed and searching. It was a little girl, her hair mussed, still in a nightgown. Fanny obviously had woken her.

"Who are you?" the girl asked curiously.

"I'm Fanny. What's your name?" Fanny was trying to engage the child on her level. She was no doubt a younger sister to Sarah.

"Glenda Marie Anderson." The little girl stated this as though she had been coached to answer this question.

"Well, Glenda Marie Anderson, is your mommy available?" Fanny asked, smiling.

The child smiled back and said, "I'll get her. She's in the kitchen making fairy's food." She said this as though Fanny would know what she meant.

She waited, nervously, wondering what "fairy's food" might be. Before she could guess at it, a woman appeared in the doorway. "Yes? Can I help you?" The woman was an older replica of Sarah. Same oval face, brown eyes, slim build.

"Mrs. Anderson?" Fanny inquired before she started her rehearsed statement.

"Yes...," the woman said, worry showing on her face. No doubt, she had been expecting this since the time Sarah came up missing.

"I'm Fanny Small, a friend of Sarah's," she began.

A hand flew up to Mrs. Anderson's mouth, tears filled the brown eyes. She froze, expecting to hear that her daughter was dead.

"No, it's all right, really," Fanny tried to allay her fears.

"She sent me to you...because I need your help." Fanny continued, "Sarah is well, but she told me not to tell you where she is. I'm sorry. I gave my word as a friend."

"Why doesn't she want me to know where she is?" her mother asked, her face showing her heartache.

"Her father. That's all I can say," Fanny said.

"Well, please," Mrs. Anderson said, pulling herself together, "come in."

Fanny followed the woman into the house. She led her into a parlor, shutting the door behind them.

"What do you need from me?" she asked Fanny.

"I'm pregnant," she began. "I need a place to stay until the child is born. I will work for my keep." She wanted to assure her of that. "I can cook and clean. Watch the younger children...whatever you need, I'll do it. Just please, don't send me away." Fanny wondered if she looked as tired and scared as she felt.

"And you know my Sarah?" Mrs. Anderson asked softly.

"We met at work. Once again, that's all I can tell you," Fanny said apologetically.

Mrs. Anderson nodded as though she already knew what line of work her daughter was in. "Of course, you can stay," conceded Mrs. Anderson. "When I introduce you to the rest of the family, I'll just say you're my niece. They don't know all of my extended family," she explained.

Fanny smiled with relief and gratitude that Sarah had been correct in saying her mother would not turn her away.

"Thank you so much," Fanny said. "You don't know how important this is to me," she wanted to convey her sincerity.

"Of course. Let me show you where you'll be staying."

Fanny followed Mrs. Anderson up a staircase into a small room. The bed was made, a spread covering it that had little roses embroidered on it. Fanny set her suitcase upon the bed, and turning to her benefactor, asked, "Do you happen to have a pair of scissors I can borrow? I've been meaning to cut my hair."

"Yes. Oh, but it's so lovely as it is," Mrs. Anderson protested.

"I need a change," said Fanny simply and realized that really was the truth.

"I'll get them for you," she quickly exited, and Fanny took in her surroundings. A bureau, certainly large enough for her meager belongings, a hamper for dirty clothes and linen, a wastebasket completed the sparsely decorated room.

She paused, and without thinking, she said to herself, "Thank God for this," and then Fanny remembered God was no longer a part of her life. The stone that was her heart reminded her of the disconnection she had brought about. If there is gratitude to be shown, it would be to Sarah and her mother. Without undressing, Fanny slid her shoes off and lay back onto the bed, which felt incredibly soft. She fell asleep before she had time to think of anything else.

❖━━━━❖

With her shorn hair, Fanny looked like another person. Her eye had reacted quickly to the treatment of wearing the specialized glasses, and she no longer had any disfigurement. Her girth increasing with each passing month, her clothes were becoming barely wearable.

Mrs. Anderson was kind enough to sew garments that suited Fanny's condition. As promised, Fanny cooked, cleaned, and babysat the children, of which there were three: two girls and a boy. Glenda—named after her father, Glen—Mary, and Glen Jr. Fanny had to speak clearly when calling either Glenda or Glen so as not to have both of them answering. Seemed silly to Fanny to name two children after the same father. She wondered if it was Mrs. Anderson's own choice, or was the father just some sort of egomaniac.

It didn't take long for Fanny to find out. She met Glen Anderson the evening she arrived. He was a massive man, or more accurately put, he was fat. Though still young in his facial appearance, he was going bald. She had extended her hand upon introduction, but he didn't take it in return. All he said was, "Another mouth to feed. Great," and he turned and walked away.

Fanny hoped she could avoid seeing him most of the time.

Fanny learned that "fairy food" was oatmeal with brown sugar and cinnamon. It was Mrs. Anderson's way of getting her children to eat oatmeal. She told them it was what all the fairies had for breakfast far away in Fairyland. Fanny learned to make up such stories in order to get the children to do many of the tasks children dislike doing. Things like washing their hands after using the bathroom, making their beds each morning, and doing their studies. She thought Mrs. Anderson quite clever to have come up with the idea.

Glen Anderson was a salesman and traveled a lot. Just as Fanny hoped, she didn't have to be in his presence very often. Being regarded as his wife's niece seemed to be a protective fact as well. She blessed Mrs. Anderson for telling this lie about who she was.

Fanny came to love the children as if they were her own. She joyfully awaited the arrival of her own child knowing he or she would be the best part of who was.

And that gave her something to look forward to.

22

Going Back Home

Time passed. Fanny knew she needed to formulate a plan for after her child was born. She had been to a doctor only once, and he was the one who worked for Lulu. She felt fine. Mrs. Anderson knew a midwife and would get her to assist in the birth. But then what? She couldn't impose on the kindness of Emma Anderson forever.

Fanny decided that she should go back to Porter's Bend. Perhaps she and Ollie could babysit for one another. She would get a job of some kind, and she would be a good mother to her child. Aunt Anna need never know the circumstances of her child's conception. At least, in Porter's Bend, she didn't have to fear Lulu coming after her and forcing her back into the business. The more she considered all this, the more sensible it seemed to her.

When her time came, the midwife was sent for, and though her labor lasted twenty-two hours, she didn't mind. She had gone through the nine months, waiting for her baby to grow and be born. The pain was only a minor suffering, and when she first beheld the face of her newborn son, she

Sandra Lumbrezer

knew it had been worth it all. He was perfect. She named him Audren George. The first name because she had read about a character in a novel and it appealed to her; the second was for her Uncle George.

She would call the boy Audie for a nickname. She told Mrs. Anderson as soon as she was strong, she and her son would be going back home. She promised to send money when she had some to pay for all the help she had bestowed upon her.

Mrs. Anderson's only request was Sarah's whereabouts. With the knowledge she wouldn't be there, Fanny told Mrs. Anderson where she could find her daughter. Fanny also warned her about Lulu and the fact that she didn't take kindly to losing employees. She told her to be careful.

Fanny sent a letter ahead to Ollie and her mother, asking them if they would allow her to stay with them until she could manage other accommodations.

<hr>

The day Fanny stepped off the train in Kingston it had been a little over a year since she had been in Porter's Bend. Her hair short and with a baby in tow, she looked like someone else. She was no longer the naive girl she was when she left.

Ollie was waiting for her at the dock on the Porter's Bend side of the river. She promptly took the baby boy out of Fanny's arms. She fussed and chattered over him proclaiming him to be the handsomest baby boy since the birth of her own son, Robert.

Ollie told her that her father had died six days after she had left. She thought knowing he did not linger long would make her feel less guilty, if guilt were an issue. Fanny said, "Let's go by his place. After all, it belongs to me now. If I can get work, I won't need to impose upon you and your mother for very long. It probably just needs a good scrubbing."

"Fanny, the place is so run down. It should probably be condemned. I don't think Mr. Small ever put any work into the place, and you know it's pretty old," Ollie reminded her.

"Beggars can't be choosers," Fanny said. "I'd rather be on my own instead of depending on others." She insisted she could manage.

The house was a sorry sight. The porch posts leaned awkwardly. Wooden boards were missing from the floor of the porch. Inside, it smelled of sickness and death. Fanny opened a couple of windows to air it out. Everything had a thick layer of dust on it.

"All right," Fanny said, "it's as I thought it would be. I'll come back tomorrow and clean the place up."

She and Ollie went back to the Reynolds's home. Vera Reynolds was exuberant at the sight of Fanny. She hugged her and took the child, fussing over him just as her daughter had done. Robert, now a big boy of four years old, came running out and, seeing the baby, asked his mother if this was his brother. Everyone laughed at this and tried to explain to him, no, the baby was just going to be a new friend for him, not his brother. They explained to him that he wouldn't be able to play with him for a long time though.

Fanny felt warm and happy inside, looking around at her friends. She hadn't realized how much she had missed them and Porter's Bend. It really was good to be home.

The next day, she went to the house she was left by her father's death. She cleaned everything, top to bottom. Ollie kept Audie so she could do what she needed to in order to make the place livable. She stood, appraising her work. It wasn't much, that was for sure. But it was hers, and it was clean.

As she walked back to the Reynolds's, Fanny noticed all the things she used to take for granted. The trees budding, the smell of honeysuckle along the path, the sound of birds singing. She came to the fork in the road, the one path led to the Baptist Church she had grown up in. A lump suddenly rose in her throat when she thought about all the times she had played with her doll under the pew while Uncle George and Aunt Anna worshipped the Lord. She took the path, and there it was.

The church had been painted since she was here last. The minister's name on the sign was no longer Isaiah Tucker. She didn't recognize the name of the new pastor. There was a saying on the sign, "Seven days without God makes one weak." She smiled ruefully at the play on words. She never thought she would ever long for the days when she was a child, but here she stood, crying as she remembered those long-ago days. What would God say to her now? He must be so disgusted with her. The pain of the past year welled up like a balloon about to pop. She felt so condemned she couldn't stand it.

She turned around and walked away from the church. She felt as though God would never accept her again. She had made her bed, and now she must lay in it. The oft repeated phrase was another sad reminder of her youth.

❦───────❦

Fanny asked around all of Porter's Bend and was able to procure work from some of the wealthier land owners. She would do their laundry, wash it, and iron it for a small sum each week. It would be enough to get by on, along with what she had left from the inheritance Aunt Anna had given her. It felt good to be doing good, honest work again. She had every intention of raising her son right. She would see he went to church too. Just because she had disowned God did not make her an unbeliever. She would send him to church even though she couldn't go herself.

That's just what she did. From the time Audie could walk, she would walk him to the Baptist church and make sure he was in the Sunday school room he belonged in, and then she walked home, and she picked him up when it was over.

Some folks thought she was embarrassed to show her face inside the church. Others thought she was mourning the loss of a husband and that's why she didn't come herself. But whatever her neighbors thought, they respected her for working hard and bringing her son to church. Everyone loved Audie. He was so sweet-spirited and really seemed to understand beyond his young years about the Lord. He was a blessing to the church.

Audie was saved at the tender age of five. He then made it his little boy mission to tell everyone he saw that Jesus Christ is Lord. He couldn't yet read, but he quoted scriptures from the Bible. He memorized them just as if he'd read them. He was truly an inspiration to be around.

His mother's heart swelled with love and pride for her son. The years of hard work were beginning to show on her still young face. When word reached her aunt and uncle that she was back in Porter's Bend and that she had a son, Aunt Anna made the trip from Jonestown to see Fanny. Uncle George was not able to make the trip; he had been ill for the past six months. Fanny had tried to prepare herself for this day, but no matter what she might have said was of small importance to Aunt Anna. Her aunt grabbed her and hugged her, crying the whole time. There was no judgment, only love.

Fanny felt she didn't deserve Aunt Anna's love, but she was certainly glad she received it. The visit wasn't long, and her aunt had to get back to Uncle George. Somehow, a weight Fanny had been carrying for a long time felt lifted. She was thankful for her aunt's forgiveness and understanding.

When new people came to Porter's Bend, Fanny would approach them with a small welcoming gift; she made a cake or sometimes cookies. Then she would offer her service to each family to take care of their laundry.

One such family was the McFields. He was an attorney in nearby Kingston, and she was a nurse. They both worked full-time and were only too happy to avail themselves of Fanny's skills. Their two children were both school age, and they worked while they were at school.

This family paid Fanny twice as much as most of her clients. She endeavored to do the absolute best she could to keep them as customers. Mr. McFields' shirts were spotlessly white and crisply starched. The same could be said of Mrs. McField's nursing uniforms.

On this particular day, after having done their laundry for several months, Fanny was preparing to deliver their clothing back to them. Fanny's back ached from bending over the washboard all day, and her arms were sore from hanging all the articles on the clothesline. She felt as though she could have slept twelve hours easily, but she knew she had to get the laundry to the McField home by

5:00 p.m. So she set out with the clothing, carefully laid out in baskets and on hangers. She used a small red wagon to transport it all.

There were no vehicles in the driveway of the McField home. Fanny guessed the two might be working late. She went through the servant's entrance and would have just left the laundry on the table in the back foyer, but as she turned to exit, a voice stopped her.

"Can I help you?" and she turned around to see who was talking.

A tall, young fellow with curly hair stood there. He wore a pullover sweater and neat corduroy pants. This was the fashion of young college men these days. She did not recognize him.

"Oh…I was…just delivering the laundry. It's all done." Fanny motioned to the clothing she had placed on the foyer table.

"Oh," the young man replied, "you must be Fanny then." He extended his hand to her. She accepted it, and they shook hands.

"Well, you have me at a disadvantage. You know who I am, but I don't know you," she said, smiling.

"I'm sorry," he said. "Of course you don't know me. I'm Bernice's younger brother, Timothy Barnes."

Fanny realized the young man to be Mrs. Mcfield's brother. Not knowing what else to say, Fanny told him, "It's nice to meet you. I'll just be on my way, then…" She edged closer to the door.

"Nice to meet you as well," he said, and he smiled. She thought he was quite handsome, especially when he smiled. "Maybe I'll see you again sometime," he commented.

"Maybe." Fanny thought it odd that the brother of one of the McFields was being so personable with a servant such as herself.

"Okay then," he said, still smiling. "Let me open this for you." And with that, he stepped around her and opened the door.

"Thank you," Fanny said, surprised at how nice he was to her.

He nodded and waved to her as she turned to go. She chuckled to herself, thinking if his sister and brother-in-law had been home, he probably wouldn't have given her the time of day.

23

Brothers

Ollie was watching her son, Robert, play with Audie. Though two years older than Audie, they played together well. They really had become like brothers to each other, just as Robert had thought when he first laid eyes on him as a baby. She laughed inwardly remembering that.

Time went so fast. *Gosh*, she thought, *I can't believe my son is seven years old. It seemed like yesterday when he was born. Too bad his father doesn't know about him.* She couldn't help regretting her emotions, allowing her to get herself caught up in Robert's father's eyes. Men could sow their wild oats and just walk away. It's not easy for the girls. Not that she would want to not have Robert with her now.

He was the love of her life now. Robert gave her what she tried to find in every man she ever knew: unconditional love. She thought it strange but cute that Audie preached to everyone. He had shared the gospel of Jesus with Robert, Ollie, and her mother. Robert listened solemnly to all Audie had to say about it and said the sinner's prayer with him. Now, they were practically inseparable.

Ollie was so happy Fanny had come back from Chicago after a year away. They could help each other with babysitting, and each was moral support for the other. Sometimes, she thought about how nice it would be if Robert had a father to be here, to be a role model for him. The only men around him were the deacons in the church. She worried that wasn't going to be enough to get him to manhood safely.

Robert wanted to go to church with Audie. She tried to explain to him that God was in their church just as he was in Audie's. He seemed a little disappointed, but she thought it was more the desire to be with his friend than anything else. Robert pointed out, and rightfully so, that he didn't get to go to the Lutheran Church all the time. So, guilt induced, Ollie had been faithfully taking her son to the Lutheran Church each Sunday. Actually, after a couple of weeks, Ollie noticed she felt better. She began to look forward to Sundays.

Fanny would never talk about Audie's father. *I'm sure she wanted a father for her son just like I do*, Ollie thought to herself. Fanny said very little about her time in Chicago. Just that things didn't work out the way she had hoped. Not wanting to pressure her, Ollie had accepted that and didn't ask her about it anymore. Fanny sure had changed a lot in the year she was there—cutting her hair, for one. Ollie would never have thought that would happen. And her eye looked wonderful; you'd never know she ever had a problem with it. She seemed so strong and confident now. Maybe a year away was just what Fanny had needed.

Ollie looked out the window. It was getting late. Fanny should be coming at any time. The boys hated being separated. She always had to reassure them they would get to play again soon. She turned and looked at the two of them. They were building a house out of Legos, and Audie was telling Robert that someday they would have a house like it and Robert could come and stay with Audie and his mom. Ollie smiled, thinking how sweet the two of them were. If she could only keep them little like they are now, never be grown men who fathered children they would never see. While lost in her thoughts, she didn't hear the front door open. Her mom's voice floated in from the other room. Fanny was here.

◆————◆

She felt bone weary when she came in the door of the Reynolds's home. Fanny asked Mrs. Reynolds if she would mind if she had a cup of coffee before she gathered up Audie and went home. Mrs. Reynolds obliged. Fanny sat at the kitchen table, sipping the hot liquid slowly, letting it drain through her. Hopefully, it would give her enough of a boost to get home. Fanny noticed a bottle of vodka on top of the refrigerator. She remembered the night she and Ollie had drank from a vodka bottle, laughing and talking about all their plans for the future.

She got up and grabbed the bottle. It was already open, so she quietly opened it and poured some into her coffee. Just enough to take the edge off, she told herself. She tried to replace the bottle just as it had been so as to avoid detection.

Just as she sat back down, Ollie entered the room.

"Long day?" Ollie asked, sitting down also.

"Definitely. What with the Morris's and Hobb's wash, I didn't think I was going to make it back to the McFields' house with their stuff until dark." Fanny had taken several sips of her doctored coffee and was beginning to feel the warmth of the alcohol coming up through her throat.

"Well, at least you know it's a steady income," reminded Ollie.

"Right," answered Fanny, not raising her eyes away from the coffee cup.

"Hey, are you all right?" Ollie could tell Fanny was not acting like herself.

"Sure," Fanny said, "I'm just a little tired."

"If you want, I could keep Audie overnight. Robert would love that." Ollie made the offer as much for herself as for Fanny.

Fanny thought about what she needed to do the next day. Mondays was Morris, Hobbs, and McFields wash day. Tuesday was three other neighbors' wash. Wednesday was three others. Thursday, she tried to get her own wash done, and Friday was still three more neighbors' wash. She looked down at her hands, red and swollen from scrubbing on a washboard. She had such nice-looking hands once upon a time. It didn't do any good to try to heal them up. She would just have to stick them back in the water.

"All right. If you don't mind, that would be great," Fanny said gratefully to Ollie. She rose and said, "I'm going to get going then, okay?"

"Get some rest, Fan," Ollie said, hugging her friend.

"I will." Fanny left the Reynolds's house wondering where and how much a bottle of vodka would cost her.

24

Hanging by a Thread

Fanny was oh so tired, but she decided to stop by the general store. It was a half a mile further from home, but she needed to make a purchase. Entering the front door of the store, the bell rang, announcing to the owner, Bill Morris, a customer was there.

Fanny scanned the shelves, her eyes going up and down each aisle, looking.

"Need some help, Fanny?" Bill Morris asked, recognizing her.

"Yes, do you carry any alcohol?" she inquired.

"Yeah. I keep it in the back so it won't walk out the door, if you know what I mean," he said pleasantly.

"Oh yes, I understand." She smiled. Then she quickly added, "It's for a cake I'm baking. The recipe calls for a cup of vodka."

"Huh, that's funny. I've heard of rum cake, but not a vodka cake." He laughed again, pleasantly.

"It's a new recipe," Fanny explained. "Everybody is making it now."

"How much would you like? Most expensive, middle, or cheap?" he asked Fanny.

"Well, I'll just take the middle one," she answered. "I wouldn't want the cake to flop because the vodka was too cheap. Just one bottle."

"Sure, sure." Bill nodded as he went to get her a bottle of vodka.

When he brought the bottle back out and set it on the counter, he said, "That'll be $3.50, little miss."

Wow. That was almost as much as the McFields' paid her to do their laundry. Nonetheless, Fanny pulled the money from her purse and counted it out to Mr. Morris. He bagged her purchase and handed the bag to her.

"How is Ben doing?" Fanny asked, hoping Mr. Morris wouldn't notice any note of anxiousness in her tone.

"Great. Doing very well. Got a baby on the way. Due in late March next year."

"How nice." Fanny smiled, trying to seem pleased for Ben. "I've really got to get going."

"Stop back sometime," Bill told her as she exited the store.

◆———————◆

She drank most of the quart of vodka that night. She fell asleep and did not wake up until a knock on her door roused her. She opened her bleary eyes, trying to focus. She had slept in her clothes. The knocking continued. When

Fanny stood up, the room seemed to be moving in circles, and she noticed her head was pounding. The knocking was still rattling the door.

She stumbled over to it and opened it. There was Ollie, with Audie in her arms. She looked at Fanny, her dress all wrinkled from sleeping in it, her hair all awry, and her eyes bloodshot.

"What in the world," Ollie said in amazement at Fanny's odd look. "What happened to you?"

She walked past Fanny, even though Fanny had not invited her in. She picked up the near empty bottle by the side of the bed.

Ollie held it up and looked at Fanny, questioning her by the look on her face.

"Yes, all right," Fanny slumped back onto the bed. "Look, I was tired and depressed," she told Ollie. "Please don't lecture me, Ollie. My head is splitting in two,"

"Well, I guess you get what you deserve," Ollie told her. "I'm taking Audie back home with me. You are in no condition to watch him. I'm going to make you coffee."

"Oh, puh-lease! How can you stand there and judge ME? You, of all people?" Fanny said, raising her head up to look at Ollie. "You were no saint either. You stopped being any fun after you had Robert." Then she laid back down on the bed, moaning in pain. Then Fanny began laughing. She couldn't stop laughing. She realized she sounded hysterical, but she couldn't make herself stop.

Ollie stood, coffee pot in hand, just staring at her. Without another word, she swept up Audie, who had been watching his mommy, spellbound. She went quickly out the door.

"Good riddance," Fanny mumbled as she turned over and went back to sleep.

◆———◆

Fanny woke up again, and the sun was setting. The mind-numbing pain was gone, and in its place was that anxious feeling she had lately whenever she woke up. She wasn't sure which one was worse. She only knew she could not drink like that again. She knew she needed to apologize to Ollie too. Had she really said those things to her?

Poor little Audie. She was ashamed she had allowed her son to see his mommy hung over. She vowed to herself never to do that again. She just had to get through things on her own from now on.

Once, she would have cried out to Jesus for help. The fleeting thought of this made her want to cry, but she fought the urge. She had to be strong. For herself and for her son. She was on her own now. Not even Jesus could help her anymore. She wasn't going to go begging anyone, not even Jesus, for help.

After drinking two cups of strong coffee, Fanny walked to the Reynolds. She apologized to Ollie, promising her it was a one-time event. She left with Audie. She tried to remember what day this was. Saturday. Right. Audie clung to her hand tightly.

"Would you like to go to Kingston today?" Fanny peered down to look at her son's tiny face.

"What will we do there?" The little boy, his big blue eyes looking back at her.

"We'll have a nice lunch together and maybe walk around and see the sights. How does that sound?" She smiled at him.

"Okay, Mommy." Audie smiled too, his face looking angelic as he asked, "Can I get a hamburger?"

"Of course you can!" Fanny bent down and picked him up and hugged him close to her.

The smell of his hair was sweet, like clover on a summer day. She couldn't help but cry, thinking that she would have to find more work just to make up for taking her son to lunch.

"Don't cry, Mommy," Audie said, patting her face. "I don't really need a hamburger."

"Oh, that's not why I'm crying," she lied. "I'm just so happy that you are my son."

"So why cry?" he asked her.

"These are tears of joy," she explained to him. "You know, you feel so happy the happy spills out through your eyes."

"Okay." Audie seemed well satisfied with the explanation.

25

Timothy

Timothy Barnes was on summer vacation from college. He was working as an intern for his uncle receiving valuable on-the-job training; this would be a star on his resume. With only a year to go before he graduated, Timothy was young and eager.

His parents wanted him to practice law; he wasn't sure what he wanted. If he chose law as a career, he wanted to help others who traditionally couldn't afford a luxury like representation of a legal professional. He would even work pro bono if that's what it took to help the less fortunate.

This mentality was met with derision by his father. "We didn't make sure you had a good education to squander it on poor people," his father had said. It was a never-ending battle.

He had only just begun the internship for his uncle when he had a conversation with his aunt Bernice. He told her how he was thinking of nursing as a career. She said he hoped he enjoyed standing on his feet for long hours and taking care of sick and dying people. He just laughed and told her that's exactly what he'd enjoy doing.

She was a nurse by profession now, but in her day, she had been a beauty queen enjoying such titles as Miss Tennessee and Miss Southern Belle.

She didn't really have the compassion and kindness usually associated with nursing. She only chose the field because her daddy had been on the board of regents at the Knoxville School of Nursing Sciences. And because if she went there, daddy would foot the bill.

Timothy was certainly happy for the opportunity to further his experience but wasn't sure how well he was fitting into his aunt and uncle's lifestyle: dinner parties, fund raising events, servants. He felt he was out of his league and had spent one evening trapped in a corner while a tipsy old man from some prestigious law firm forced him to listen to his life story. It puzzled him why he needed to be a part of these gatherings. But his uncle insisted. It was how people got to know you, how you gained clientele: word of mouth.

Timothy didn't know how to convince his father that he didn't want to be an attorney. Why did fathers always have to push so hard? His father had been a blue collar worker, working his way up to a foreman position. His father didn't even go to college. He wanted everything to be better for his son. He did understand, but he still wanted to find the niche he fit in by himself. So long as he did honest work, what difference did it make?

Maybe he *should* study for another line of work; he would like to become a nurse and was sure he'd be very good at it. His father laughed when he mentioned that possibility and told him, "Men aren't nurses, only women are nurses."

He knew none of this would be easy. Maybe after the summer was finished, his father would listen to him. Timothy thought he would just bide his time, get through the internship. Then, he would confront his father.

26

Chance Encounter

The Saturday lunch trip to Kingston was well worth what Fanny paid for it, just to see Audie so cheerful and easily delighted with everything. The only bleak spot being when Audie said he wished Robert could have accompanied him. Maybe next time, his mother had assured him, knowing full well there would be no next time any time soon.

It had been another long day. She had to deliver the washed, starched, and ironed items to her customers. Finally, she only had the McField laundry left to deliver. She pulled the wagon behind her. Her steps had slowed down considerably from when she started.

The back door was open, as usual for her use. She picked up the basket and walked in.

"Here, let me help you with that." The same young man who had spoke to her the week before came and held the door open for her. Then he took the basket of laundry from her hands.

"So," he said, smiling, "We meet again."

"Yes," replied Fanny, not sure what to say.

"Can I offer you some lemonade?" he asked. "You look like you could use it. Not that you look bad...or anything." He looked at her.

For the first time, Fanny noticed his brown curly hair, strong facial features, and engaging smile.

"Oh...I don't think I should," Fanny said, thinking the elder McFields wouldn't look kindly upon their nephew talking with the help.

"Of course you should," he insisted. "Come here." He walked into the kitchen area. He reached into the icebox, pulling out a tall pitcher. He poured two glasses.

"Here you are." He handed one of the glasses to her. "Please, sit," he said, and pulled out a chair from the table for her to sit in.

"Are you sure that the...I mean...your aunt and uncle would care if I'm here...like this?" Fanny asked softly.

"Like what?" he asked, looking innocent. "Like a hardworking woman who is thirsty?"

"Well, I guess when you put it that way," Fanny said, grateful for the wonderfully cold lemonade.

"What other way is there to put it?" Timothy asked her.

"You're very considerate, Mr. Barnes," she said, drinking down the remainder of the glass.

"And you can call me Timothy," he answered. "Bernice is my aunt, so my last name is Barnes."

"I probably won't see you again to be calling you anything," Fanny said, standing up to leave.

"Don't be so sure," Timothy said, following her to the door. "You never know what a day will bring."

"Well, thank you for the lemonade," Fanny said, and she started for home. The lemonade had been just what she needed to give her a second wind. She smiled as she pulled her empty wagon down the road.

<hr />

Life was settling into a very familiar pattern: work, deliveries, dinner, bedtime, over and over again. Fanny had long since given up her dreams of living in a fine home or traveling far beyond the confines of Porter's Bend. She had learned to accept her circumstances. She was too old for pipe dreams. Audie was getting to be a big boy. He now was enrolled in school. First grade. He was naturally a smart boy, and she was proud of him.

Then one evening, when Fanny had finished the last of laundry deliveries, Ollie came running to meet her when she walked in the door.

"Fanny, you won't believe what has happened!" Ollie's face was glowing, she was so happy.

"What? Tell me," Fanny couldn't help but smile in response to Ollie's joy.

"I'm getting married! You won't believe how it happened. A man came into the dress shop where Mama sells her dresses. The clerk said a man had come in asking about me. She told him I lived in Porter's Bend. He left a phone number and she gave it to me. I thought there wasn't much chance that it would be Robert's father, but it was. I told him all about Robert. He got discharged from the navy and he got married to someone else. But he said he never forgot about me. His wife died from some illness." At this point, Ollie waved her hand as though it was a minor detail in the story.

"He was amazed and wondered why I had waited so long to get in touch with him. He said he was so happy to have a son and that he was coming next week, and we are going to get married! Can you really believe it?"

Fanny stood there, taking it all in. She felt as though she was hearing Ollie chatter on about this man named Robert also, but she had a roaring sensation inside her ears and had to shake herself mentally to hear what Ollie was saying.

"He's got a home in Rochester, New York, and he's taking us with him to live there!"

"How wonderful," Fanny said, but in truth, she was thinking, *How will I get along without Ollie?*

She tried to push aside the shock of the news. She told her friend, "Ollie, I'm happy for you. Really, I am."

"I know, isn't it wonderful?" Ollie twirled around and did a little dance.

"Yes, it really is," Fanny said, trying to sound cheerful, but something in her face gave away her true feelings.

"Hey," Ollie said, taking her friend's shoulders in her two hands, making her face toward herself.

"We'll still see each other sometimes. And we'll write to each other too. It'll be fine."

Ollie suddenly thought about not just what she was gaining but what she would lose. She grabbed Fanny, hugged her, and started to cry.

Fanny realized she had taken her friend's good mood and ruined it, making her think of other things.

"Look, Ollie. I know all that. Really, I think it's wonderful news. I wish you both all the best," Fanny smiled, and this time, she was sincere.

"I'm really gonna miss you, Fan," Ollie said, tears still in her eyes.

"I'll miss you too," Fanny answered, thinking to herself, *More than you can ever know.*

27

Losing a Friend
and Gaining Another

Robert Palmer was still the same as Fanny remembered him. He just looked a little older and, hopefully, wiser. Fanny smiled as Ollie reintroduced him. Mrs. Reynolds was there of course. She couldn't seem to stop crying. She insisted they were just tears of joy. Fanny couldn't help thinking that separation from her grandson was more likely the cause.

The ceremony was simple; the minister of the Lutheran Church presided. After a short reception, the two were off for a brief honeymoon at the Kingston Ridgemont Hotel. Beyond that, the family would no longer be part of the Porter's Bend community.

Audie took the news of Robert's leaving hard, but as he later told his mother, "Jesus told me not to worry. He said He would take care of him."

Once this had been revealed to Audie, he was no longer agitated in his spirit. If he looked sad or cried, he assured his mother that it was only because he was missing his friend, not because of worry.

Audie was always saying things like that, which amazed his mother. He said Jesus watched over them while they slept.

"Yes, I know," Fanny would reply in a tone meant to appease him.

"No, Mama, I see Him. He stands right here." And he walked to the foot of the bed he slept in to show her.

Sometimes, he said he saw angels too. Like when Robert, Ollie, and his father were getting onto the boat to Kingston, Audie said he saw an angel in front of them and another following behind them. Fanny just stared at him. She really couldn't understand, but she couldn't say it wasn't so. She had to believe him.

Audie's bedtime prayers would last well into the time Fanny had drifted off to sleep. She would wake up and see him, across the room, still kneeling, whispering his requests to God. She could only sigh and wonder how her own son could be so faith-filled when her own faith had withered away.

Fanny still believed in God. She just didn't think He paid any attention to her anymore.

Somehow, Fanny got through that first week without Ollie, then a month. Before she really had time to think about it, a whole year had passed. Mrs. Reynolds kept Fanny updated on her daughter. She told Fanny that Ollie was looking into furthering her education. Fanny thought, "The world still turns. Everyone else had a life that was going somewhere, everyone except for me."

This was not what she had planned when she remembered her childhood. Fanny loved Audie, that was true. The rest of her life was just swallowed up with work and figuring out how to survive. Was this all there was ever going to be for her? The more she tried to block these troubling thoughts, the more they seemed to dominate her thinking.

Audie was in second grade now. Her life was literally passing her by. Such were the thoughts in her head the day she walked into the McField house with the usual delivery of finished laundry. Fanny had bumped into the nephew a few times since that first meeting. Their conversation was casual, but lately, they had taken a more personal turn. Timothy asked Fanny about her hopes, her aspirations. He listened to her and told her some of his own.

She felt a little disappointed that she didn't see him around. *Well, why should he hang around and wait for the laundry girl?* she thought to herself. That's all she was, after all. As she walked down the path away from the McField house, she heard a male voice call her name.

"Fanny!"

She turned around and there he was, walking toward her, smiling. He was dressed as if he was going to the office or just had left there.

"I thought I'd missed you," he said. "You're earlier than usual." He came beside her, grinning.

"Yes, I got an earlier start today," she said and smiled back. She was pleased to note he had kept track of when she came.

"I'll walk you home, okay?" he asked.

"Don't you have more important things to do?" she asked him, motioning to the suit he wore.

"Not at the moment," he answered. "You know, I enjoyed our conversation so much the last time, I wanted to continue it." He sounded very genuine.

"Oh," was all Fanny could think of to say. She suddenly felt nervous.

"What's wrong?" he asked, noticing a change in her demeanor.

"Oh, nothing. I just wondered…why are you interested in talking to me?" She looked at him, their eyes meeting.

"I just…think…you are a nice person, and I'd like to get to know you better."

"And…say, you get to know me…what then?"

He turned his head and said deliberately, "I don't know…I guess we'll have to wait and see."

"Hmmm," she said.

"All right," he said, "to show you my intentions are honorable, would you like to have dinner with me tonight?" He held both arms out to his side, palms up and open, in a gesture of openness.

"Are you serious?" she asked, thinking he probably wasn't.

"Totally serious. I'll even wait while you get ready."

"You really want to take me out to dinner?" she asked, her insides beginning to tumble around, thinking she might actually be going on a date with Timothy. Barnes, the nephew of one of the McFields!

"I wouldn't ask if I wasn't serious," he said in mock offense.

"All right then. I will get ready."

"I'm in no hurry," he responded, and they walked together down the path.

28

Love Finds Fanny

At six years old, Audie Small had developed a relationship with Jesus that many Christians could envy. He not only prayed, he just talked to Him. Some could argue we all talk to Jesus through prayer, but with Audie, it was so much more. When he told his mother that Jesus was with them, he meant it in the most literal sense. Even seasoned evangelicals who conversed with the youngster would sometimes look upon him as though they disbelieved what they heard.

Audie told everyone he met about Jesus. He was totally sincere and perhaps because he was young, folks listened intently. He had more than a few converts. When he questioned his mother about her church attendance, Fanny was quiet for a moment. She had known this question would come about, but just didn't know when it would be presented.

She wanted to say something that made sense to a child without sounding as though she was an unbeliever. Finally, she settled on one sentence:

"I don't feel that I belong there any more, Audie." she said.

"But, I think everyone belongs in church, Mama." he said, looking up at her with his sweet face. "It's God's house."

"I know, honey. It's…it's…complicated. I'll explain it all to you when you're a little older." She hoped he'd forget about this question soon enough.

"All right, Mama." Audie knew he couldn't argue with his mama. Jesus wouldn't like that. Her answer did perplex him. Jesus didn't want anyone to feel out of place in His house, he reasoned. He would talk to Him more about it. Jesus would work it all out, he was sure.

<hr>

The restaurant Timothy took Fanny to was elegant. Fanny felt conspicuous in her common flowered frock. It was her best outfit, but she couldn't help but feel inferior somehow as she sat admiring the other female patrons with stylish clothing she was certain were very expensive.

The menu items were listed in beautiful script and the prices! She couldn't believe anyone charged so much for one meal! Timothy told her to order whatever she liked and not worry about the cost, but Fanny felt a tinge of guilt eating food that cost as much as a whole day's wages.

She decided on braised chicken breast. Timothy had steak. When she took the first bite, Fanny thought she had never tasted anything so grand.

"You enjoying yourself?" he asked her, his eyes meeting hers over the table.

"Oh, yes!" she replied. "I'm just not used to anything so nice as this," she waved her fork around in a circle, indicating the atmosphere.

"Well, it would be a shame for a lovely woman like yourself to be deprived of fine 'nice' things." He smiled boyishly.

He really did look like a little boy, she thought to herself. His curly brown hair and impish grin were very attractive to Fanny.

Maybe that was how it started. The conversation went from polite chit chat to something of a more personal tone. He placed his hand over hers and told her she was beautiful. He gently touched her face and it felt like a fire ignited inside of her. She heard an inner voice telling her to be careful, but she brushed it aside.

Somehow, the two of them were in one of the hotel rooms that the restaurant was part of. Fanny knew she should have been stronger, more disciplined. All her womanly desires had been pushed down for so long, she couldn't help but give into Timothy. In the brothel, it had become mechanical. This felt different. He made Fanny feel wanted, and not just the physical thing; he made her feel loved.

When it was over, she said,

"I…you probably," she stopped, unable to finish her thought.

"What is it?" he asked, turning her toward himself. "What's the matter, Fanny?" His eyes seemed so caring, so concerned.

"You probably won't want to see me again. You think I'm some kind of cheap floozy now. How can you respect me now?" She had her face downward, unable to meet his gaze.

"What are you talking about? I'm not a cad, after all. I don't take with that old Victorian caste system!" he sounded like he meant all that he said. "I've had some better opportunities in my life than you may have had, otherwise, you and I, we're the same." He tilted her chin up so he could look into her eyes.

"Really?" she asked him, desperately wanting to believe him.

"Really. Now, let this be the end of that sort of talk. I'll leave first, out the back way. I wouldn't want your reputation to be tarnished in any way," He laughed and the way he looked, Fanny laughed also.

"Thank you, Timothy," she said quietly.

They said a final goodbye and Fanny raced to pick up Audie from Vera Reynolds' home. Vera had encouraged her to take her time, enjoy herself. Vera believed Fanny was having dinner with a female friend, but she didn't want to take advantage of her kindness. Vera always said Audie was a joy to babysit anyway.

Timothy was happier than he had been in some time. He was glad to have someone like Fanny to 'spend' time with. She was smart and funny and not too bad to look at. He knew his aunt and uncle, and of course, his father, would not like it if they knew. They wouldn't want him 'consorting' with the lower class. Well, he'd just have to make sure they didn't find out. He was quite certain Fanny would not be one to share their rendezvous.

His father had everything worked out for Timothy. He would fulfill the internship with his uncle, go to work in the Edward's firm of attorneys in Bristol. It was a high profile firm that dealt in corporate law; a position guaranteed to make Timothy a wealthy man.

Elizabeth Edwards was the daughter of the senior partner in the law firm. Timothy had met her at various times throughout the past years. He found her attractive and educated, but boring. She was very strait laced too. Another boring aspect of womanhood, especially in Elizabeth's case. She wasn't the type he would have chosen for himself, but arguing with his father was pointless, he knew.

For Fanny, the night at the Ridgemont was the first of many trysts she shared with Timothy. Fanny thought she had never felt so light, so free as she did when she was with him. In fact, she thought nothing could have made any of it any better. Except perhaps, a declaration of love from Timothy that would end with a wedding band on her finger. Yes, Fanny was in love. Just thinking about him made her heart race. She found she smiled much more.

She kept smiling right up to the time she realized she was with child. At first, she felt panicked. Then, she began to see it differently. Timothy would certainly want to marry her and give his child his name! Of course, her days of endless drudgery were almost over!

"Everything is going to be perfect." she said to her reflection as she pressed her dress flat against the bump on her abdomen. She just knew it.

29

Disappointment

She was already in the hotel room when Timothy arrived. She tried to calm herself. She didn't want Timothy to think she was crazy. Her face was flushed, her mouth dry. She drank a glass of water. It did little to appease her nerves. She put her hands behind her so he would not notice they were trembling.

When he walked in, she was poised on the edge of the bed. She rose, smiling.

"You look exceptionally lovely," Timothy told her, kissing her mouth and then her neck.

"Timothy. I made special arrangements so we could spend the night together." She looked at him, expecting him to be pleased.

His shoulders slumped at this piece of information. She could tell he was not expecting this.

"I thought…I hoped…you would be pleased." She fell back down on the edge of the bed. "Obviously, I was wrong," she said, her head dropping in disappointment.

"No, it's not that," he said quickly. "I didn't bring a change of clothing. My aunt and uncle expect me to be home at a certain time."

"You're a grown man! What do they care when you come or go?" she asked, sounding somewhat petulant.

"There's more to it than that, Fanny. They are old school, they don't think that way. If they even suspected we were together like this, they might…," he stopped, searching for the right words.

"What?" Fanny began to feel angry. "They might think I'm not good enough for you, is that it?" her voice was steely.

"No, of course not," he said as he tried to soothe her ruffled feelings. "But if they tell my father, I will be shipped right back home."

"Oh," Fanny's quick anger began to retreat. She certainly didn't want him to have to leave.

"Why…how…why does your father's opinion matter so much? You are an adult, after all." Fanny was beginning to have second thoughts about telling him about the pregnancy.

"He doesn't," he reassured her. "It's complicated."

"I wanted to tell you something tonight. Now I'm not sure you'll want to hear it." She couldn't look in his eyes, fearful of what he might say.

"Well, let's have it then. Tell me, please!" He pretended to pout.

"All right," she conceded, and taking a deep breath, she said, "I'm pregnant."

The air in the room seemed oxygen-deprived as Fanny waited for his reaction.

His face was unreadable, and then he began to laugh. Fanny exhaled, believing against all hope that his laughter was a good sign. He pulled her to him, clasping her tightly. It would be all right after all, she thought with relief.

"That's wonderful, Fanny. Don't worry, I will take care of everything." He looked into her eyes, saying, "I'll pay for the doctor, the midwife. I'll provide whatever is needed."

Fanny felt fear begin to creep over her.

"So…we are…getting married." It came out as more of a statement than a question.

"Sure we are," he said, "just not right away."

"Why not? If you are happy to be a father, what's standing in our way?" Fanny asked him in bewilderment.

"Fanny," he began, "not everything is so cut and dried. I have my father, my aunt, and uncle to contend with. It's going to take time. I'm going to do the best I can under the circumstances. It's going to take time to…prepare things."

"I really thought we would get married right away." She knew the disappointment showed on her face and she didn't care.

"Please be patient, Fanny dear," he implored.

"I can't see how I have any other choice," she said flatly. She stood and said, "I'm leaving now. There's no point in my staying here alone." Fanny picked her overnight bag up and walked to the room door.

"I'll take care of the hotel bill, don't worry about that," he said.

Fanny thought, *It doesn't matter about that. It's the least of my worries now.*

She answered, "Fine. I'll see you next week, I guess."

She had developed a lump in her throat, and she didn't want him to see her cry. She walked out the door quickly.

All the way back home, Fanny cried. People stared at her, but she didn't care. Her disappointment was too deep, her pain too real. She managed to stop the tears by the time she reached the house. A flat, emotionless apathy settled down upon her in the place of sadness.

She decided to wait until time to pick up Audie. Vera Reynolds wasn't expecting her until tomorrow evening. *What a mess I've made of my life*, she thought. She fell asleep, exhausted from all the drama of the evening.

By the next morning, Fanny felt somewhat better. She told herself, *Timothy did say he would take care of everything.* That did serve to ease her mind. And he didn't say they would never get married; he just said not now. She managed to make herself feel content and hopeful for the future with these thoughts. He was a good man. He would do the right thing by her. She was sure of it.

30

The Proposal

As expected, Timothy went to see Elizabeth Edwards. He knocked on the door of the Edward home and was greeted by a servant who showed him to the sitting room in the mansion.

He entered the room and marveled at the opulence of the place. As he was admiring all of it, Elizabeth entered.

"Timothy!" she said, smiling.

He turned and took the hand she proffered. She smiled back at him and said, "Sit down." And she sat down on an overstuffed sofa patting the spot next to her.

He sat and said, "I wanted to see you…" Timothy wasn't sure how to proceed. It seemed rude to just jump into "would you like to get married" right away. He hadn't seen Elizabeth in almost a year.

She seemed to sense his awkwardness. She laid a hand on his arm and said, "It's all right. I spoke to your father earlier." She gave him a knowing look.

Timothy exhaled. "I'm so glad," he said. "I didn't want to appear as though…you know, making a business deal. It's not all about the money for me, I hope you know that. I've always liked you and thought you were a nice girl," he said all this in one breath, not making eye contact.

"I understand," she replied. "I like you too, Timothy. So…did you have something you wanted to ask me?" She cocked her head to one side, teasing.

"Oh!" he said, suddenly understanding her meaning. "Would you like to marry me?" He had a rather sheepish look on his face as if he didn't know her answer.

"Yes!" she laughed and threw her arms around his neck with so much force he fell back against the sofa. He laughed along with Elizabeth.

So the two became engaged.

31

Elizabeth

The rest of the week passed slowly for Elizabeth. She remembered Timothy Barnes as a handsome young man with impeccable manners. It was delight she felt when her father told her he was interested in seeing her with matrimony in mind. Although she was considered a beauty, no one as yet appealed to her in a romantic sense. Timothy appealed to her father in the business sense, and that made the young man doubly attractive. She was determined to not let him get away.

Timothy remembered Elizabeth as tall and slender with a classic beauty. She carried herself well and spoke well. She would make an excellent hostess at dinner parties. It would be a fine match. He couldn't complain about the arrangement. The Edwards were known for their philanthropy throughout the state. They would certainly encourage him to help others less fortunate.

And so, their engagement was set, but it was agreed upon that it would not be announced until later. They didn't want to start unnecessary rumors that their engagement was made for ulterior motives.

From the time they became betrothed, Timothy began spending his weekends in Knoxville. Elizabeth had grown up there and still lived in the home her parents shared. It was a large house, some would say a mansion, so her privacy was not an issue.

Elizabeth's family had been brought up as Catholic. Gerald Mcfield had not been to a Catholic church in years. Her mother went to mass weekly and observed all the holy days. She wanted her grandchildren raised as Catholic. Elizabeth wasn't so worried about these things. She would let her mother give any future children their spiritual education. What mattered to her was having a man of stature and class, someone who would accompany her to the symphony, the ballet, and the country club. Of course, he must be generous and kind also. Timothy seemed to fit all aspects of the man Elizabeth wanted. And he wasn't hard to look at either.

When Timothy came on the weekends, they spent hours talking about his wish to one day enter the medical field as a nurse or perhaps a doctor. Nursing is what he really wanted so he could be more hands on with people. She admired this noble desire to help others. He told her that once he had acquainted himself with working for her father, he wanted to begin schooling in nursing. She thought that he had lofty ideas. She didn't understand why he couldn't just be contented as a well-paid attorney. It wasn't as though he had to worry about making less money. Her father had plenty to go around.

Timothy did not talk about his relationship with Elizabeth to Fanny. He felt it was unnecessary for her to know. She wouldn't understand. He felt real affection for Elizabeth as a woman; she was everything he needed to be successful. Fanny was someone who fulfilled all his other desires. Elizabeth had been raised to be a lady; he could never expect her to be what Fanny was to him.

He was very content with his life as it was. A beautiful woman who adored him that agreed to be his wife and a sweet woman with a heart of gold who would do anything for him to function as his girlfriend.

<hr>

As months passed, Fanny grew larger. She did her best not to gain a lot of weight. She watched her diet and ate only healthy foods. It wouldn't be good for either her or the baby if she ate like a horse. Her pleated skirts hid her condition effectively. She looked robust and healthy.

She was perplexed, however, with Timothy. Whenever she was able to catch a few words with him, she would ask him when he planned on telling his father about the two of them. He always reassured her it was going to be soon. She longed for the days when they seemed so close and happy. Would they ever return? These were Fanny's thoughts during her pregnancy.

She knew she must be patient. Timing was so important with something like this. And he *had* bought her that lovely boxed set of lace handkerchiefs. They came in a gold box, with her initials on them. He said he got them in Knoxville when he was there on business.

Audie was growing up so fast Fanny felt as though he was getting taller right in front of her eyes. He was becoming more involved in church, spending two to three nights there a week. He started holding healing services one night a week. During these services, he and other pastors laid hands on the sick and prayed for them. Often, they were healed immediately. News of the young boy who had the gift of healing spread throughout the region.

The church was having difficulty housing the many who showed up for these healing events. They had to schedule the services in two, sometimes three, different services to accommodate all the folks that came for prayer. Fanny was proud of her son, but at the same time, she felt anxiety. Would God punish her for what she had done? She willingly lay with a man she wasn't married to; now, she willingly carried his child. This, she felt, was just one more sin added to her long list of offenses. How long would God turn a blind eye? She suffered a great deal of guilt but hoped He would not hold her sins against her unborn child.

Fanny continued to do her laundry work just as she had before she became pregnant. She grew tired more easily, but other than that, she felt fine. No one would have thought anything was different. She could feel the child in her womb moving, and she smiled to herself, hoping she would have a girl this time. She also hoped she would have her father's good looks. It shouldn't matter if folks could connect the looks of child and father. Surely Timothy would set things straight by then, and they would be married. If they suspected she had been pregnant before the marriage, well, that would be just gossip.

After Fanny reached her sixth month, her cheerful attitude began to wane.

32

The Cold Hard Truth

The new day Fanny awoke to was bright and sunny. It made everything seem a little better. She needed to get some things from the store, so she readied herself for the task.

She needed the fresh air she breathed as she walked the path to the Morris General Store. She wished every day was as beautiful as today. Bear Mountain was awash with color from the arrival of the autumn season. The leaves crunched underfoot with each step down the gravel path. She went over her list of necessities in her head, trying hard not to forget any of them.

She entered the store, still repeating the items to herself. Two local women were at the counter, talking low with the store owner. Fanny walked down each aisle, collecting in a cart all that she needed. She strained her ears to hear the conversation from the front of the store.

"Yes, it's true," the one lady insisted, with a wave of her gloved hand.

"So when is the big day supposed to be?" the other asked.

"Well, *I* heard it's going to be announced at the country club dinner before Thanksgiving."

Ben Morris interjected. He was a country club member, so of course, he would know.

Fanny wondered who it was that they were discussing so rabidly. Bunch of gossips, she told herself. You'd think they had better things to do. She only listened in, she rationalized, to make sure they weren't discussing her.

"I hear it's what his father and her father want to happen. Not so sure about how Timothy feels about it," the one lady commented.

Fanny's heart beat faster as she heard the name she was so familiar with mentioned. She walked closer down the aisle to hear them better.

"She's very pretty. He couldn't find a better looking girl if you ask me."

"Well, I think it's time Timothy Barnes got married. A young man like him needs a woman to keep him in line."

Fanny mused, so it is Timothy they are talking about. And most certainly it was not Fanny they were linking with him. Her heart was beating so fast she thought she might faint. She steadied herself by holding onto the shelf of items in front of her.

"Miss, Fanny?" Ben Morris's voice broke through the roar of blood coursing in her ears.

"Are you all right?" He sounded concerned as he watched her, noticing that she looked suddenly pale as she gripped the edge of the shelf directly in front of her.

"Oh, I'm fine," she answered, hastily. "I'm just a little dizzy."

"Here," he said, and produced a chair from behind the counter. The women were both staring at her with a sudden change of interest.

"No, really, I'm fine." She forced herself to stand up straight and smile.

The women at the counter said their good-byes to Mr. Morris and left. Fanny let a sigh of relief escape her lungs.

"Those two"—He laughed, glancing her way—"they sure do love to wag their tongues." He said this as though he had not participated in the gossiping.

"It's the nature of people," Fanny said flatly, accepting the proffered chair. She tried to quell her racing mind, to somehow make sense of what she had just heard. Surely they were mistaken about Timothy. He wouldn't do such a thing. Would he? She was struggling with all the racing questions in her head.

"Well, you just rest here as long as you need," Bill told her kindly.

"Thank you," Fanny replied. "I'll just be a couple of minutes."

"I'll ring up those items you have there while you rest," he suggested.

"Yes, that's a good idea."

Bill rang up her purchases and bagged them. Fanny paid for the items and walked back home, in no hurry to reach there.

———◆———◆———

Today was the McField laundry day. Fanny wondered if she would see Timothy when she dropped it off later. She desperately wanted to talk with him. If he wasn't there, she wondered how she could get a message to him. She scrubbed the nursing uniforms while mulling over this thought. Suddenly, she thought to herself she would write a letter with no return address, mark it "confidential" and send it to the law firm in Kingston that Timothy's uncle owned. Yes, that would work.

She wanted to do it right away, so she stopped her scrubbing and dried her hands on her apron. She found pen and paper and sat down at the kitchen table and began to write. She put the date on the paper and held the pen aloft, wondering if she should just say he needed to see her immediately and that is was an emergency situation, or should she just flat out say what she had overheard, demanding an explanation. She settled for the first one, afraid that if there was any truth to the accusation, he might very well avoid her completely.

She quickly wrote what she needed to say and placed it in an envelope. Now getting it mailed without suspicion.

Being a rural post office, it would be a short time before all of Porter's Bend knew Fanny Small had sent a letter to Timothy Barnes's office with no return address.

The clock said it was 1:15 p.m. Audie would be home from school around 3:30, and the post office was open until 5:00 p.m. She would send him and advise him not to answer any nosy questions. It was difficult for Fanny to wait the two and a half hours until school was dismissed, but she had no choice. She tried to keep her mind on the laundry, but her mind still reeled from the overheard conversation at the store.

At last, the time came, and her son walked into the house.

"Hi, Momma," he greeted her, smiling as usual.

"Sweetheart, I need you to run an important errand," she said this seriously, looking Audie straight in the eye.

"Sure, Momma. What do you need me to do?"

"I need you to take this to the post office right away. Tell them it needs to go out as soon as possible."

"Why are you writing to a law office? Are we in some kind of trouble?" he inquired of his mother innocently, reading the address on the front of the envelope.

"No, no...nothing like that. It's just that I need to get the deed for this property verified...in case...I might need to sell it." Fanny was amazed with her ability to form a lie so quickly and with such ease.

"Do we have to move, Momma? I like it here." Audie started to sound upset, thinking he might have to leave the place he had lived all his life.

"No, honey, I mean...someday, you know, when you are all grown up and probably move away yourself."

"I'm never leaving you, Momma," he stated this firmly and she knew he meant it.

She stepped close to him and wrapped him in a tight hug. Whatever she may have done, Audie was the one thing she had done right.

"I'm so lucky to have such a good boy," she said, still hugging him. "Now take this, and here's the money for postage." Fanny gave him some coins. "And hurry! The postal vessel will be loading up by 4:30."

"Yes, Momma." Audie took the letter and left to go to the post office.

⬧————⬧

Two days later, Timothy knocked on Fanny's door. One look in his eyes was all she needed. With all the will she had to keep her voice calm, she told Audie to go outside while she spoke with the guest. Audie looked puzzled but went outside obediently.

"It's true, isn't it?" She had turned her back to him. She couldn't bear to look at him when he said it.

"Yes, it's true. But I can explain," he said, laying his hands on each of her shoulders.

"Oh, well, if you can explain," Fanny turned around to face him, anger boiling up inside her, her voice dripping with sarcasm. How did he think he could explain his engagement away?

"It had to be this way. Both Elizabeth's father and my father had this merger planned long before you and I ever met. I should have told you right away, but I didn't think things...would progress to this state of affairs." He sounded contrite, remorseful.

"Well, it has," she answered, sadness and disappointment evident in her voice.

"I know and I'm sorry. But it doesn't have to be a bad thing, does it?"

"What are you talking about? You are engaged to another woman! I'm not supposed to see this as a bad thing?! Why don't you just slap me in the face? It wouldn't be any more painful!" she sobbed into her hands.

"I mean...," he struggled to say the right words, "Elizabeth is...someone who is a figure head, someone to play a part...it's a business arrangement."

"So...you don't love her? It's a marriage that's to be in name only?" She turned, looking at him quizzically.

"Pretty much, yes." His eyes downcast, he asked, "Do you understand? Are we all right then?"

"It's certainly not something I would have chosen," she said, "but if there is no other way, I guess I'll have to get used to it." She said this, knowing she would never be able to get used to it. "I guess we never will get married and have a family now."

"No, no...don't say that." He pulled her closely. "After an acceptable time, I'm going to divorce Elizabeth, and then..." He tilted her face to his and smiled. "Okay?"

She was so hungry for affection from him she threw her arms around his neck, "Of course, whatever you need me to do, I'll do it," she said, feeling the warmth of his neck against her cheek.

"Wonderful. Listen, I have to run now. I've got business to attend to," he disentangled himself from her arms, edging toward the door.

"When will I see you again?" she asked, feeling desperate for him to commit to something with her.

"Soon, I promise," he gave her one last smile and then he was gone.

Fanny slumped into a chair and sobbed.

Audie saw Timothy leave and came inside. He stood just inside the door and watched his mother, head on her arms, crying as though her heart would break. It would not be the last time he saw her this way.

33

Jane Anne

Vera stayed at Fanny's home until she felt like getting up and moving around without help. Fanny decided to name her little girl Jane Anne. Jane because Audie liked the name, and Anne for her Aunt Anna. She knew her aunt would be pleased to know she had a namesake.

"It's sad that she won't know her father," Fanny said wistfully as she gazed at her daughter's little face.

"You don't know that for certain," Vera replied with an encouraging tone though she thought Fanny was probably right. "Are you ready to talk about that?" she added.

"Well…" Fanny looked at Audie and then back to Vera. Vera understood that Fanny didn't want to discuss it in her son's hearing. Vera nodded. Since it was a Saturday, Audie was home from school.

"Sweetie," Vera said to the boy, "would you do me a favor?"

"Sure, Miss Reynolds," Audie answered in his amicable style.

"I need a small bottle of vanilla extract," she told him, handing him some change. "Mr. Morris knows the kind I use."

"All right." Audie left to run the errand.

Fanny began the story of how she became involved with Timothy. She managed to tell most of it without any tears, but when she got to the part when he said he would be there for her, her eyes began to fill.

"I've been right where you are, Fanny. It will get easier with time, it really will."

"I feel so stupid…I believed him," and the tears flowed.

"You are not stupid, Fanny. We all want to be loved and to love. Something good will come from what you've experienced," Vera predicted.

"I think it already has," Fanny looked down at Jane Anne, so small and innocent. "It already has."

34

Letter from Jimmy

Not long after Fanny's last meeting with Timothy, a letter arrived in the mail written by Jimmy's wife, Sharon. She said Uncle George was ill; the doctor believed it was cancer. She also mentioned Aunt Anna was not doing well either. *Well, they aren't young any longer,* Fanny thought to herself as she read on. Her heart was already broken. Nothing could hurt her now.

Brokenhearted or not, Fanny still ached as she read that the two people who were the most important in her life were sick and probably were dying. Sharon hinted that she was kept quite busy with the care of her own three children and that any help Fanny could provide she would greatly appreciate. Of course, Fanny knew Sharon had no way of knowing what was going on in her life. She said Jimmy made a good wage at a local factory, so if Fanny needed train fare, it could be arranged.

Fanny read and reread the letter. She desperately wanted to see her aunt and uncle. She just couldn't see how she could go to Jonestown now. She would have to take the children, and what would they think of her? She didn't care what Jimmy or Sharon thought. It wasn't any of their business anyway. But Uncle George and Aunt Anna...

Fanny mulled over the situation in her mind. She had not heard so much as a peep out of Jimmy or Sharon in all this time. If they truly cared anything for her, she reasoned, then why hadn't they communicated through Vera Reynolds? Jimmy knew she was good friends with Ollie. Or sent a message through Ben Morris at the general store? Uncle George and Aunt Anna wouldn't be around much longer. She sat and cried, frustrated and filled with despair.

Why had God allowed such good people to suffer so? He was punishing her through her aunt and uncle. Her head ached, and her nose was stuffy from all the crying. She would have prayed for them, but she didn't believe God was listening to her prayers anymore.

Fanny's tears were as much for herself as for her aunt and uncle. It would be obvious she wasn't married if she took the kids with her. Nothing had changed in Fanny's life since they left to live with Jimmy and Sharon. She just had two children to care for. She loved Timothy and wanted to believe he loved her too. Was he just playing her for a fool?

If only Ollie was here. At least she'd have her to confide in. She missed her friend so badly. She started crying all over again, bemoaning her friend's absence. *This is ridiculous*, she thought to herself. *This isn't going to accomplish anything. Stop crying and get up and DO something*, she said to herself.

So Fanny got up out of her rocking chair and made herself a cup of tea. The warmth of the beverage felt soothing going down her throat. She began to feel renewed strength, and she knew tomorrow would be a better day.

35

The Healing Touch

The service was starting. Audie stood on the platform at the front of the church. Standing upright to his full height of four feet, he was the shortest and youngest among the several that was there with him at the front of the church. At only eight years of age, Audie had already made himself a strong fixture among the elect of the congregation.

He had been in prayer for two hours prior to the opening of the service. The place was packed, he thought joyfully as he looked out over the pews. Joyful he was, but not for his own sake. Audie was joyful that so many were here to receive a healing touch from Jesus. Even if some of them didn't know Him as Lord and Savior, they had enough faith that He would have mercy upon them and heal them. That, Audie believed, was enough to open the door to salvation for those folks.

Music swelled as a trio of women singers began a praise and worship song. Audie's voice joined in the chorus. The next song set all the hands within the building to clapping, the sound of "amen" echoed through the midst. The Holy Spirit came in and was settling down on Audie and others.

Audie knew when the Holy Spirit was present. His hands began to shake with His power, and sometimes it would overtake his tongue. He had brought forth prophecies in languages even he didn't understand. Another person would stand as the Spirit brought forth the interpretation. What a great gift God had bestowed upon him. He wept with humility and gratitude.

The pastor stepped forward and asked the people to turn their Bibles to a certain scripture dealing with Jesus's healing power. He explained the scripture in simple terms and told of many of his own personal experiences with that same power. After a half an hour of sermonic speech, the pastor exhorted all those with the need for healing in their bodies to come forward to the altar for prayer.

The aisle crowded as folks made their way to the front of the church where the altar was. The pastor and other deacons, including Audie, stood in front of each person, anointing them first with oil then praying over each of them. Words of supplication, some shouted, some whispered, were being spoken unto the throne of God. Many people formed a line in front of Audie, wanting his prayer to be said over them. Everyone had heard that Audie was a divine healer, able to call upon the name of Jesus with stunning success.

Tears flowed freely among the people. If a stranger entered this place, surely he would be overwhelmed with the feelings of love and sweetness that permeated the atmosphere. It was a blessing just to walk through the doors.

When everyone there had been anointed and prayed over, Audie felt exhausted both mentally and physically. It took so much out of him he felt as though he could barely stand up. He knew he had reached the throne of God. Many would later testify that they had been healed miraculously. It was wonderful to listen to all those who had been touched by the Master's hand.

If only his mother would come. If only she would give her life over to Jesus. Audie would be the happiest of the happy. She told him she was a believer, but she wouldn't come to church. God had hidden the reason from him, whatever it may have been. Audie wouldn't stop praying for her; he would pray until his dying breath, if that's what it required. Nothing was more important to him than his mother's salvation.

<hr />

While the birth of his baby sister amazed Audie, he didn't question his mother about how it all came about. An astute student of the Bible, he had read about "begetting," so he did realize that women bore children as part of the punishment because Eve sinned. He just didn't understand the finer points of the subject. He took it for granted God took care of the details.

He was fascinated by his sister's little wrinkled face, her tiny hands and fingers, her little toes and miniature ears. He could see the wonder of God in every thing about her. He loved her instantly. He constantly asked to cradle her, gazing at her as she slept. His mother scolded him not to hold her so often, saying she didn't want to spoil her. Fanny reminded him that Vera Reynolds would have to care for her when Fanny worked and he was in school. She didn't want the child crying to be held all the time.

Audie reluctantly allowed Jane to sleep in the blanket-lined box his mother used as a bassinet. Nonetheless, he spent a lot of his spare time looking over the makeshift cradle, watching her small chest going up and down with her breathing. He felt he needed to protect her from any evil thing that might come upon her.

Three days after giving birth, Fanny had to return to work. She couldn't afford to go without working any longer. Audie went back to school, though he tried to talk his mother into letting him quit so he could go to work too. He could take care of Jane if she didn't want him working. Fanny refused both ideas. There weren't a lot of material things she could give her children, but as long as an education was free, he was going to go to school. Once again, the two of them settled into a routine of working, eating, and sleeping. Fanny's only bright spot was when she was able to pick up her baby daughter and wait until

Audie came home from school. She loved Audie with all her heart, but she felt a special love for her daughter.

As springtime beckoned, Jane grew to a sitting-up stage and looked at her surroundings with large grey eyes. A cheerful baby, she laughed and cooed with each new discovery to her world. On a free day, Fanny took the baby along with Audie on a picnic into the woods near their home. She came to the small clearing she used to frequent as a young girl. There she used to sit on the creek bank, thinking and talking with Jesus.

Fanny remembered what talking to Jesus was like back then. It was such a sweet time of refreshing herself, a cleansing of her thoughts and heart. It was like being with an old friend. Jesus was someone she could be herself with; she didn't have to say how she felt because He already knew. Ollie was an old friend, but the relationship she once had with Jesus couldn't compare to an earthly friendship. It was, she realized, because He was so many spiritual things; her Savoir, God the father, God her brother, God the best friend. He was so much more than she could have ever hoped to have with a friend on this earth. Thinking those thoughts made Fanny sad, so she struggled not to allow herself to do that.

Instead, she tried to focus on the beauty of this natural hideaway. She looked through the dappled sunshine coming through the treetops. She sat down, cross-legged, with Jane in her lap. It was still cool enough that the insects had not emerged from their hibernation. She drank in the smell of the earth, the frogs, and fish smells of the creak and thought about her life.

Audie was holding his little sister's hand and talking to her softly. His face became pensive, and he asked his mother, "Mama, will Jane grow up like me, or will she stay a baby?"

"Of course, silly. All babies grow up eventually," she replied to her son's question. She looked at Audie, who seemed so serious, "Why do you ask?"

"Well, if she stayed bein' a baby, I'd know I could take care of her. It will be harder to do once she gets older," he said, with a wise expression.

Fanny sighed and wished Audie didn't have to carry these sorts of worries upon his little shoulders,

"You know, honey, it's not your responsibility to take care of her. Right now, it's mine, and by the time she's older, she will be married, and then it will be her husband's." Fanny sincerely hoped the answer comforted him.

"I want to take care of her," he said and added, "just like I want to take care of you, Mama."

"Well now, you might just feel differently in a few years," she replied to him, thinking wistfully about her own future.

"No, I won't. I'll always want to be with you and Jane," Audie spoke firmly, his lips set straight in determination.

Fanny looked at her son with a soft expression and said, "You are my sweet, dear little man." Her hand reached out and brushed the sandy hair from his forehead.

"We should be getting back, dears," she stood, holding onto a squirming Jane.

The trio strolled leisurely back up to the gravel pathway. It had been a really good day. As long as she didn't think too far beyond this day, she could maintain a cheerful outlook. She had long since given up grieving the loss of Timothy. He didn't care about her after all. She had been a fling for him, someone to ease his manly desires. It was now something from her past, and she had to leave it there.

36

New Events

Progress was coming to Porter's Bend. It was 1926, and the flapper fad was in full swing. The Kinston Times was full of flat-chested girls with bobbed hair wearing fringed dresses and little caps that matched. Of course, none of these trends reached Porter's Bend outside the pages of the newspaper, but the folks there knew changes were coming. The local women gasped when reading about the speakeasies and the kinds of folks that frequented them; the local young men admired the bootleggers that brought the liquor to them driving cars with souped-up engines as they outraced the authorities.

Such was the world when the Holden River Bridge was built across the watery route, making transportation into Kingston much more convenient. The bridge was built in response to several drowning deaths caused by folks using canoes to reach the city. Some others had thought they could swim the distance and died trying to do that.

Fanny began to think about Vera's advice about seeking employment across the river once the bridge was completed.

It was an hour's walk, but so what? She wouldn't have to worry about money for the ferry or asking someone to row her over in their boat. It would be wonderful to never have to do laundry other than her own family's, she thought. Fanny could sew very well. She didn't know if she was good enough to get a job sewing, however. She wasn't like Vera who could make a dress out of her head without even a pattern. She could cook and clean though, so perhaps she could get a job at a big hotel as a maid or a cook in an upscale restaurant. There were so many opportunities just over that bridge!

Fanny was still a young woman, not yet having celebrated her thirtieth birthday. She was strong in body and mind. The idea of working at a new career excited her. This could change her family's lives for the better. She became determined to do her best at whatever job she could get across the bridge in Kingston.

She set out for her job hunting in a dress borrowed from Ollie. She had let her hair grow since she had cut it short a year earlier, and it already hung down the middle of her back. She swept the long hair up into a twist, hoping for a sophisticated look. Ollie did her makeup, something Fanny had not used since returning to Porter's Bend.

Ollie gave her a light touch, just enough to bring out Fanny's best features. As Fanny viewed herself in the mirror, she felt as though she was ready to take on the world.

Once in the city, Fanny walked in and out of what seemed like countless establishments. She filled out countless applications until her hand ached from writing. She used the general store's phone number as a contact. That was closer to her home than Vera's. Besides, she hated to impose on Vera for yet another favor. She already did so much for her.

She was so happy to have Ollie around for the time being. Ollie was a godsend because Fanny was encouraged through her friend. She really needed that; she had spent so much time downcast with no one to turn to.

She again remembered the days when Jesus had been her source of comfort and encouragement. Now, she felt as though a high wall had been constructed between the two of them and she had no power to scale it. Ollie kept her from feeling so alone.

Fanny knew she had Audie and Jane too, and they were a bright spot in her life also. She would have gladly given her life for either of them, but her children couldn't share her concerns the way Ollie did.

Audie seemed so sad lately, Fanny thought. He had been so excited about seeing his friend, Robert, again. Something had changed in the friendship they shared before Ollie and Robert's father had moved away. Robert wasn't the same as Audie remembered him. He had become a sullen, silent young man. He seemed bored with everything in life, including Audie. He had also picked up the habit of smoking and some language that Audie was repulsed by.

Audie was most troubled by the way Robert would answer his mom and dad when they spoke to him. Robert was smart-mouthed and disrespectful. Audie would never have dared to speak to his mama like that, but then, he had never wanted to say anything that was disrespectful. How had this happened to Robert? They had been like brothers, and now, Audie felt as if Robert was a stranger.

Audie tried to talk to Robert about Jesus, but Robert quickly rebuffed the attempt.

"It's stupid, believin' in that garbage." That was Robert's thoughts on anything spiritual.

Audie asked, "Why do you say that?" He hoped to get Robert talking about what had happened to him to harden his heart.

"Jesus hasn't helped me any," was his reply. "When I had to go to the school in the city, everyone pushed me around. I either could take it and be a wimp or I could push back." Robert gave Audie's shoulder a push to emphasize what he said.

Audie felt unprepared to deal with Robert's problems. He tried, the best he could, to explain to Robert that Jesus would have been there. If Robert had only called upon Him, he assured him Jesus would have helped. Nothing he said seemed have any effect. Audie knew he was in a battle fighting to save his friend's soul, but he would storm the gates of hell if necessary in order to achieve victory.

"People don't always live up to expectations that are placed upon them," his mother said. He didn't know she was speaking of herself as well as Robert. She said there were other boys, that he would make other friends. Audie knew she was trying to comfort him, but he was not going to let this go, not while his friend was in danger of losing his soul.

A month or so after Fanny had pounded the pavement of Kingston, Ben Morris sent word from the general store that she had a message. A restaurant named the Red Door called and wanted to meet with her about a position.

Fanny was elated! She made arrangement to meet the head chef and left the children with Ollie. The chef liked Fanny, and after talking with her, he offered her the job. She shook his hand heartily and thanked him profusely, parting with the words, "You won't be sorry, sir! I'll work so hard for you! You won't be sorry you gave me this wonderful opportunity!"

Fanny smiled the whole way home. The sky was bluer than she had ever noticed it to be, the sun felt warmer, everything felt light, and filled with hope. She hadn't experienced hope in a very long time. Folks passing by, smiled too. She was exhilarated.

At home, everyone shared her joy over the new assignment. Vera got out cake and poured glasses of milk to celebrate. If everything went as planned, Fanny would begin the next week working as sous chef for the Red Door. She could hardly wait to start a new phase of her life. Maybe God wasn't so mad at her after all.

37

All Things for Our Good

One day, at Vera's house, Fanny glanced at the Kingston newspaper lying on the kitchen table. Thumbing through the pages, there it was! A large photograph of Timothy Barnes and Elizabeth Edwards, arm in arm at some ritzy affair. She had to admit, they looked really good together. She imagined what her life might have turned out if she had been the one beside him. She pushed the thought out of her mind quickly, knowing such thinking was of no value. It was a thing of the past. She needed to be thinking of her future.

When Jane began to walk, Audie asked his mother if he could take her with him to church. She reminded him he would have to watch her the whole time, and what about his responsibilities as a deacon-in-the-making? He was expected to be up front, ready to pray for those in need.

Audie said he would, he just would take Jane with him. He wanted her to learn all about Jesus. Now was the time for her to start. Fanny sighed. She knew this time would come, and she wasn't sure just how to handle it. She felt enough guilt as it was, now she was going to be doubly guilt-ridden. At last, she relented. All right, he could take her, but only on Sunday. He didn't have to take her every time he was there. She would still learn about Jesus once a week.

Audie accepted his mother's terms, though he would really have rather had his sister with him every time he entered the church. He would take what he could and be grateful.

So it was that Jane grew up familiar with the way of the church. She happily crowed the hymns right along with everyone else. Audie let her bang away on the church organ before and after services, hoping she might have a natural inclination to play the instrument. Jane was the delight among ladies attending church, each of them offering to play with her while Audie was praying over folks. It worked out very well. Audie was admired and respected for being such a responsible and loving brother, taking the spiritual growth of his sister so seriously.

Audie was happy having Jane with him. His heart was still heavy with the burden he carried for his mother. He never ceased to pray asking God to touch her heart. He would never rest until his mother was saved.

38

Starting to Heal

Audie and Robert spent time together during Ollie's visit to Porter's Bend, not usually by Robert's choice. If Fanny needed Ollie to watch the children, of course, they were together in the same house. Robert would either stay hidden in a bedroom or go for long walks.

Audie would not let Robert isolate himself. He would stand outside the bedroom door, talking to Robert, not sure if his friend was listening. He would follow Robert on his walks through the woods, careful never to lose sight of him.

Finally, after several days of this, Robert turned, midstride between the trees, and faced Audie.

"What do you want from me?" Robert asked, his voice angry and demanding.

"Nothing," Audie said calmly. "You're my friend. I just like being with you."

"We are NOT friends anymore!" Robert practically spat the words out. "Can't you get that through your head?!"

"No, I can't. You were always like a brother to me. You don't stop loving someone in your family just because they move away. And you are part of my family." Audie said this, with simple honesty.

Robert shook his head and stood quietly for a moment, staring at the ground. Then he shrugged his shoulders and said, "Well, if you are that thick-headed, I can't help it. But don't think I won't hurt you if you keep this up."

"I'll take my chances." Audie grinned at Robert.

Unexpectedly, Robert's face broke into a smile as well. He turned and continued his walk.

A few feet behind him, Audie followed.

◆————◆

The day came after a couple of weeks of Ollie's arrival she announced that she and her husband had to leave for home. Of course, Robert would go home too. Audie was distraught, thinking he was just making headway back into Robert's life. He begged Ollie to let Robert stay with his grandma.

"I don't know, Audie. He's so strong-willed, I don't think Mom could handle him. We can barely make him go to school or do his chores," Ollie said to him, compassion in her eyes for what Audie was trying to do for his friend.

"I know…but I think I can help him. He can go to school with me, and maybe he'll go back to being like he used to be, "Audie presented his case for his friend as compellingly as he could.

"You have to let us discuss it with one another and with Robert," Ollie said. Inwardly, she doubted Robert would even want to stay with his grandma. He would probably just view it as a ploy to unload him on someone else. "And don't forget about my mom. She has to agree to this too," she added, thinking, why would she want to have an obstinate, disrespectful kid living in her house?

"I know," Audie assented. He had already determined that this would be a major item in his prayers. If it were meant to be, Robert would stay in Porter's Bend.

"Try not to pin your hopes on this, Audie." Ollie touched his shoulder, wishing she could help him understand.

"I'm not," he answered, but he knew that Jesus would not let him down.

39

A Second Blessing

Fanny happily went to her new job with high hopes and a willing attitude. The chef was that had hired her conducted a tour all around the establishment. A tall, large man named Harold, he explained the workings of the kitchen. He pointed out each piece of equipment they used and told her the importance of speed and quality. The two processes must mesh, he said. He also told her that the appearance of the foods served was ninety-five percent of how a guest would perceive the dish, whether good or bad. A well-presented plate would not outweigh poor taste however. Fanny shook her head in understanding as Harold explained all these facets of food service.

It was all new to her, this making food that was beautiful *and* good-tasting. She had only ever focused on the taste portion in cooking at home. Audie was not picky; he generally ate whatever she put in front of him.

Harold wore a white, spotless chef's coat and a tall white cap. Fanny wondered how he managed to stay so clean working with food all day. She marveled at the plates of steaming foods he put in the serving window all garnished and fancy. She wondered if she would ever be able to do the same.

She was presented with a uniform; a white button-up blouse with a white flared skirt. She was shown to the restroom for kitchen workers where she changed into the outfit. They kept white cotton aprons handy by the dozens, so a dirty apron could be quickly replaced with a clean one.

Her first duty was chopping vegetables for the dishes on the menu. By the day's end, Fanny thought she had never chopped so many onions, celery, and carrots in her entire life. What's more, they had all been used as fast as she produced them! Not to worry, Harold assured her that she would soon be speedy enough to get a head start on the next day's worth of chopping vegetables. She wondered if that was really possible for her to accomplish.

The one thing she was sure of, she was going to learn as much as she could from Harold. The better she became and the more versatile to all the duties in the kitchen would certainly increase her value to the restaurant. That was Fanny's ultimate goal.

She quickly adapted to her chopping, and Harold was proved correct; her speed steadily increased with each passing day she worked. She liked all her coworkers, who were friendly and helpful, and seemed to genuinely like her in return. She was very happy with her new job.

One day, she found herself so engrossed in her work she started singing to herself. This was a habit she had inherited from Aunt Anna, who always said, "A tune would make any chore lighter." Harold told her to turn up the volume, that he wanted to hear what she was singing. Embarrassed by the attention, she stopped singing. "You don't have to stop. It's sounded nice," Harold encouraged her.

"I guess I didn't think anyone was listening," she said somewhat shyly.

"Why would you think that? You have a nice voice," he told her.

Fanny beamed within with the compliment. She had really been lucky to have found this position. She got to work the dayshift and had her evening free to spend with the children, which she loved. And it sure did beat scrubbing clothes until her hands were red and raw. Yes, she had been very lucky. She didn't know if He was listening to her, but she thanked God for the door He had opened for her.

◆———◆

Audie withheld his total joy when Ollie told him they had all agreed to allow Robert to stay with his grandma—on a trial basis, at least. If he caused any trouble, her mother would ship him back to New York.

He had known all along that Robert would be staying; Jesus would never let him down when he was praying for a lost soul. In truth, Robert had told his mother and father he wanted to stay behind. He had heard them discussing the possibility and stepped forward to say he wanted them to let him do that very thing. He promised them he would behave himself, evening offering to swear to it on the Bible if they wanted.

Robert couldn't help but soften to Audie's constant attention. No one back in New York cared about what happened to him, besides his family that is. It was nice to feel cared for. He remembered his earlier friendship he and Audie had enjoyed and wanted to experience that again. He didn't have to pretend to be someone he wasn't around Audie. He could just be himself, and that was good enough. In New York, he had to be like everyone else, or at least pretend to be. After so long pretending, he started to *be* someone else. Now, the pretense could be dropped once and for all.

He no longer locked himself away or tried to avoid time with Audie. They did things together, like kicking around a ball in the yard or climbing a tree to look over the treetops at all of Porter's Bend. They even ventured up the side of Bear Mountain. Of course, Audie's mom and Robert's grandma didn't know this. Surely they would have put a stop to it before they started. But it was therapeutic for Robert. The physical exertion to climbing over the rocky crags freed something within his heart, allowing him to be honest with himself and with Audie.

Audie listened to Robert as he talked about the resentment that had built up inside of him when his mother got married. Yes, he was glad to have a father, but it was hard being thrown into city life and especially a city school. Everything there had been radically different from life in Porter's Bend. It had been a big adjustment. He felt as though he never wanted to go back there but realized it was probably only a matter of time before that happened.

His friend urged him to pray about it. Let Jesus back in, he told him. As the two boys sat on a high ledge on Bear Mountain, Robert renewed his commitment to God. A weight he had carried for a long time seemed to fall off his shoulders, and a peace settled over him. He was so glad he was right here, right now. He felt that everything would work out with God's help.

They climbed back down the mountain just before the sun set, and when Robert looked to the west, he thought he saw Jesus standing with outstretched arms, welcoming him back into his presence.

40

Jane Comes Home

With the advent of the Holden River Bridge, things were changing around Porter's Bend. Folks noticed an increase in the number of strangers who came across from Kinston into their town. Perhaps, it was curiosity that brought some of them. Previously, if you couldn't afford boat fare, you could have swum the expanse. Since the distance was a good three quarter mile of water, excellent swimming skill was a must-have. It had been the death of some, unable to make the trek, succumbing to a watery grave. Still, others came to hunt and fish in the fertile and abundant river and surrounding woods. Whatever the draw, the foot traffic increased throughout the region, causing concern for the folks who lived in Porter's Bend.

Ben Morris benefited from the folks who wandered through the community. Many stopped at his store to purchase a drink or something on their way in or out. Of course, he had to keep his eyes open for the unsavory ones who were not above pocketing what they could not or would not afford to pay. His income became larger and enabled Ben to close the store on Saturdays and do some fishing himself.

There was also some talk about wealthy folks from beyond Kingston developing homes and businesses, thereby expanding the borders of Porter's Bend. This met with talk of petitions among the current land owners. When Timothy Barnes knocked on Vera Reynolds's door seeking her signature for this very issue, she readily agreed to sign. She had been very grateful Fanny had been at work when he showed up. Though Fanny never said she had any relationship with Timothy, Vera had her suspicions. For one, Jane had the same curly red hair and blue eyes. How likely was that, seeing Fanny had not been any where outside Porter's Bend prior to Jane's birth?

While he was getting Vera's signature on the petition, Timothy mentioned that he had heard Vera was an accomplished seamstress.

"Why, yes, I've made my living that way for about thirty years now, she answered."

"Would you consider making my fiancée's wedding dress? She is very petite. I'd like to have the best possible dress made for her," he explained.

"Of course," Vera willingly agreed to the task as the sum of money offered would buy groceries for the household for at least three months. So it was that Elizabeth Edwards's wedding gown would be made right there in Porter's Bend.

Vera told Timothy, "Please tell Elizabeth to contact me about the dress details." Vera hastily scribbled her phone number on a small note and gave it to Timothy.

He promised he would do that very thing.

"I'll make sure she calls you very soon. Vera hoped she could manage all this when Fanny was not around just to avoid any awkward situations for either of them.

Elizabeth did call Vera the very next day. Since Vera's schedule was open during the weekdays, Elizabeth arranged a midweek meeting. Elizabeth arrived at Vera's door dressed in a beautiful suit with a hat and shoes that matched. She really was an elegant lady, Vera found herself thinking.

She escorted her client into the sitting room and asked her to sit.

"What kind of wedding dress are you considering?" Vera asked.

"I love the Victorian era style," Elizabeth said, smiling. "I want something tasteful yet…"

Elizabeth paused, looking for a word to describe the dress she envisioned.

Vera nodded and drew the outline of a wedding dress and together, seamstress and bride- to-be, designed the wedding dress.

"Thank you, Mrs. Reynolds," Elizabeth offered Vera a gloved hand when all was the arrangements were in order.

"You know, if this turns out as I hope, I'll make sure Timothy gives you a sizeable bonus."

"I'll certainly do my best for you, dear."

Elizabeth turned as she reached the door. "It will be more than worth it. After all, a girl only gets to be a bride once in a lifetime."

Vera smiled and thought, *Not all of us.*

Now, Vera thought, if only she could keep this quiet and away from Fanny's knowledge, all would be well

41

The Mission Field

Though the loss of love she experienced with Timothy was painful, Fanny was able to replace that longing with her newfound independence. She derived a sense of fulfillment and self-worth. Excelling at her work became her new focus.

That focus did not go unrewarded. Harold spoke to the owner about Fanny's increasing skill, and as a result, she was promoted. She now had the title of assistant chef and a thirty-cent raise in her pay. Alas, with more responsibility and money came the relinquishing of her personal time. Fanny was expected to be present for all events the hotel hosted: various seminars, speaking events, and other venues. Fanny dutifully complied with their needs, even if it meant working longer hours and being away from her family on holidays and weekends. This was a small price to pay for all the benefits she enjoyed with the job.

That was why, one Saturday, Fanny found herself leaving work after the sun had already set on the summit of Bear Mountain. She forewarned Vera to not expect her at any given time. Her employers liked her to leave quitting time open-ended.

It was a warm, sultry twilight night Fanny walked through to reach the Holden River Bridge. That much of the way home was a two-mile walk and another three-quarter mile beyond that. The street lights cast long shadows as she passed beneath them. Once out of the business district of Kingston, the amount of pedestrians dwindled perceptibly. She was ever so thankful for the air-conditioned working areas of the hotel. The sweat was already running in rivulets down her neck unto her back, and she had only just finished a little over half of her normal route.

Some folks in Porter's Bend were well off enough to own a vehicle. Fanny had many other priorities on her mind to take care of before she could even begin to contemplate that type of purchase. Occasionally, a neighbor heading over the bridge would offer her a ride. She was always glad of such opportunities, since she would be on her feet, working the rest of the day.

Many folks walked the two miles over the bridge into Kingston. It was not unusual to see all manner of people traversing the bridge back and forth across the Holden River. A few youngsters even fished off the bridge during the long, lazy summer days. For the most part, Fanny didn't mind the walk and, in fact, enjoyed it. The warm summer air, the sunshine on her face all made the trip to her job most pleasant.

This evening, it was not quite what she was accustomed to when walking home. She couldn't help but feel just a little fearful as she came to the sparsely populated part of town just prior to the bridge. She wasn't used to being outside of Porter's Bend at this time of day, but she tried to convince herself that she had nothing to fear now that wouldn't have been there during the light of day.

Fanny had just passed the last house along the route when she noticed the footsteps behind her. She tried to tell herself that it was no one, and if someone else were about at this hour, they were probably just getting out for the stillness of the twilight air. Nonetheless, she quickened her pace. The footsteps seemed to match her step; she stepped, they stepped, step, step, step. What should she do, she wondered? Should she try to run, should she scream for help? No, no, calm down, she cautioned herself sternly. Just nonchalantly turn around and look at who is behind you.

Fanny stopped, with the pretense of looking in her handbag. The footsteps behind her stopped also. She turned and looked behind her. It was an elderly woman, walking with a cane. The woman carried a parcel, no doubt from the grocers'.

"Nice evening," Fanny offered, by why of conversation.

"Still hot," the woman returned, not sounding as if she care to be talkative.

"Yes, isn't it?" Fanny felt relief wash over her and was glad she had stopped and taken out her handkerchief, with which she wiped her neck and face.

The old woman proceeded on her way past Fanny until she was out of sight.

With a sigh, Fanny kept walking. It was now completely dark. No street lights beyond this last one she passed under. The bridge was unlighted as was most of Porter's Bend beyond the occasional lighted window or security light of residents who lived there. The moon was bright and the stars twinkled above the heavy warm night air. They provided all the light she had to see where she stepped. *Oh, well*, she said to herself, *there's no reason to be afraid. I'll just walk as fast as I can to the Reynolds's house. Maybe Vera will let me stay the night since it is so late.*

Fanny stepped unto the bridge, her shoes making what seemed like a deafening sound in the still night air broken only by the chirp of crickets and the croaking of bullfrogs. The bridge arched up in the middle, making her body work harder on the incline, but she scarcely noticed. She quickened the pace as she walked with all the intensity she was able to exert. Finally, she reached the crest of the bridge. Now the easy part, the downhill side. The downgrade slant forced her to slow down so she did not stumble and fall down the side of the bridge like a rolling pebble.

There it was, the foot of the bridge. Not a single lighted window. Maybe it was later than she estimated. Perhaps, it had taken longer than she realized, after all, she *had* stopped to speak to the old woman.

Everything looks different in the dark, she mused. Just as she started down the pathway she had walked a thousand times before to the Reynolds's home, a figure loomed directly in her way. She took her breath in sharply, caught unawares.

"Howdy, ma'am," a man's voice said. She thought hard, but recognition of the voice was not forthcoming.

"Good evening," Fanny answered, sidestepping to go around the figure.

"Hey, now," the man said, stepping in front of her to block her way again.

"What do you want?" she asked, her voice was shaky. She made an effort to control it.

"Why, I jest wana letle comp'ny, is all." his voice sounded coaxing, as if he were attempting to get a shy dog to come to him.

"I don't have time to be of company to you right now. I have to pick up my children," she made an effort to push past him, but he grabbed her arms, one hand over her mouth. She was screaming inwardly, fighting to push him away from her. His hand over her mouth felt suffocating, and she struggled to breathe. She dropped her purse as he manhandled her, dragging her off the path unto the grass alongside it. Then it felt like a rock hit her hard on the side of her head as his fist came down upon her. The darkness in which the two tussled became utterly black as Fanny was knocked unconscious.

When she woke up, her mind felt hazy. She had no clue how long she had been there.

The glint of sunlight through the trees had somehow penetrated her eyelids and woke her. Her head felt like it had when she drank a whole bottle of vodka. She managed to raise her arm to her head. That was when she felt something sticky on her forehead. She looked at her hand. It was cut on the palm, but the fingers that she had just touched herself with were wet with her own blood. She felt as though every bone in her body ached. She tried sitting up. She got as far as propping herself on her elbows when she realized some of her clothing about her ankles. Her uniform skirt just covered her private parts. She was nauseated.

She retched in the grass next to her. With all the strength she could muster, she pulled her underwear up and over her knees to cover herself. She cried, knowing she had been violated in the worst way a woman could be violated. She tried once more to stand, but her legs gave way and she landed in a crumpled heap in the grass.

She looked at her surroundings. About one hundred feet away was the path she was on the night before. If she couldn't walk to reach it, she would have to crawl. She made her way forward, stopped, started, stopped. It was an exhausting effort. Each time she stopped, she would collapse, her breath coming in hard, short blasts.

Once reaching the pathway, she crawled along beside it toward Vera's house. Thank God it was the first house on the pathway into Porter's Bend. If she could make it there, she would be all right. She knew if she could just get to Vera and her children, she would be all right. *Please, God, please God, help me!* she screamed the phrase over and over in her mind.

Vera Reynolds was passing by her front window when she glanced down the path. Something made her freeze in her steps. She moved closer to the window and drew aside the curtains. She didn't know who it was, but she had a horrible feeling she did indeed know who it was. She yelled to Audie as she raced out the front door, "Watch your sister!"

Vera ran as fast as she could to the figure of the woman who was crawling along the pathway.

"Fanny, Fanny!" she shouted the name as she got to Fanny's side. Vera knelt down in the grass and pulled Fanny up on her knees. She collapsed onto Vera's shoulders. Their eyes met, and Vera screamed as she looked at the blood, partially dried, on the one side of her friend's face. Her chef's jacket had been torn, her legs bruised and scarred.

"What happened to you?" she held Fanny and cried with her.

"I…coming home…it was late. It was dark…a man… He…" Fanny's voice choked off with the deluge of tears that shook her body.

"Shhh. It's all right now." Vera held Fanny's head against her shoulders, patting it. Vera's tears wet the top of Fanny's hair as she held her, soothing her.

"I'm here now. You're safe." Vera helped Fanny to her feet, and putting her weight against Vera's frame, she managed to walk slowly.

Inside the house, Vera led Fanny into her bedroom, shutting and locking the door behind her. She then stripped the torn chef's coat and skirt off Fanny. She washed and disinfected the cuts with peroxide. She put one of her own clean nightgowns over her head and pulled it down around her, gently putting Fanny's arms through each armhole.

Vera placed a pillow beneath Fanny's head. She covered Fanny with the quilt and left her to rest.

❖━━❖

Vera was thankful to the Lord that Audie had been in the other bedroom she had converted into a nursery, playing with his little sister. That he hadn't been a witness to the state his mother was in when Vera helped her inside.

Now, Audie came into the kitchen where Vera began making breakfast for him and Jane. Robert was already at the table eating.

"Where's Momma?" he asked.

"She's resting. She was very tired. She wanted to see you and Jane, but I told her I would tell you she said" hi'. She really needed to lie down." Vera sounded as convincing as she could, hoping her red eyes or taut expression would not reveal what she was thinking and feeling.

"Oh, okay," Audie said, sitting down at the table.

Thank you, Jesus, for making Audie such a good boy, Vera said to God as she made the eggs and toast and set before him.

"Was your sister awake?" she asked him, hoping to distract him from looking too intently at her.

"Yes, she is. She's playing with her stuffed bears," Audie told her as he made short work of the food.

"Don't bother your mother, mind you," Vera said to Audie. She turned to go get Jane out of her crib in the other room.

"No, ma'am."

Once again, Vera lifted her eyes heavenward and thanked God that he had spared these children the loss of their mother.

42

Joy and Trials

It took less than twenty-four hours for the news of what had happened to Fanny Small to spread through the community of Porter's Bend. Husbands and fathers expressed anger and outrage, vowing to hunt down whoever it was that dared to do such a thing to a well-known resident and neighbor. Women of all ages made sure they did not walk anywhere without someone to accompany them. They felt there was safety in numbers.

Mothers wouldn't let their children out of their sight when they played outside, fearful a similar fate would befall them. The fear permeated onto the children; they would go running into their houses when an unfamiliar face strolled by. Everyone felt uneasy after what had transpired.

Vera Reynolds suggested Fanny inform the Kingston police of what had happened to her. Fanny didn't know if she should. She couldn't remember too much of what happened. She could barely see his face in the darkness; what she remembered was the smell of him: a sweaty body odor combined with tobacco and alcohol. She would never forget that smell. It was certainly enough to make her abstain from drinking any alcohol the rest of her life. And the smell of cigarettes made her nauseated.

She was grateful she had been unconscious for the actual violation. She didn't know if she could have lived with the memory of it. She knew she couldn't go back to the hotel job. She would never walk alone on the streets of Kingston or across the bridge that linked the city with Porter's Bend. There was no one she could depend on to take her or go with her, so she had no choice but to resume laundry service for folks around the community of Porter's Bend.

Fanny couldn't understand why she was always having to face continual set backs in her life. She knew everyone faced adversity, but somehow, it seemed she suffered more than her share. Would it always be this way? Since her attack, she slept little. When she did sleep, it was a nightmare-filled sleep that swirled about her mind. A dark road, a faceless man, and she was running, running for her life in a deep blackness all around her. She would wake, sometimes screaming, her heart pounding as if it was ready to leap from within her chest.

Vera insisted she stay with her and Robert until she was better, physically and mentally. Fanny did not argue with her. She busied herself helping Vera with sewing, caring for her children, and wondering if folks would allow her to do laundry for them again.

The days passed by slowly through the lingering days of the summer. In a little less than a month from now, school would be in session for the children again. Fanny knew she must begin finding work to bring in an income soon. She couldn't rely on Vera's kindness forever.

With the boys accompanying her, she went home to home throughout the Bend, asking folks if she could take on their laundry duties for a small sum of money. Most of her old customers were pleased to have her back, then she came to the McField residence. She didn't know if she could bring herself to knock on their door. Of course, Timothy was probably not around anyway. No doubt, he was in Knoxville with Elizabeth.

This was her thinking when she rang their doorbell, the only home in the Bend that possessed such a device. A housekeeper answered the door. Fanny explained why she was there. The housekeeper said she would pass on the information to the lady of the house. Fanny thanked her, and she and boys went back to the Reynolds's home.

Vera suggested Fanny offer to cook meals for folks as well as do laundry. After all, she had learned a great deal while working under Harold's supervision. Why waste the talent? Fanny agreed but didn't think these poor folks could pay her for cooking *and* laundry services. She would just mention it in passing, in case anyone wanted her to do that for them.

It wasn't long after Fanny returned to doing laundry that she was approached to cater an affair. While picking up the wash at the McField's home, Bernice McField stopped her before she walked out the back entrance. She said, "Miss Small, I understand you've had experience with catering. I spoke with the owner of The Red Door. He tells me you're quite good at hosting and catering events." She waited expectantly for Fanny to say something.

Fanny was surprised and pleased to know her former employer had given her such a glowing reference. She answered, "Yes, ma'am. I do have some experience in that area." She looked down at the bundle of laundry she held in her arms, not feeling as though she could meet Bernice's gaze, wondering what she might be thinking.

"Well, my nephew is getting married at the end of September. I thought I might recommend you to his fiancée, if you're interested, that is."

Fanny sighed, knowing full well it was Timothy's wedding.

"I mean, I'm sure they'll make it more than worth your time and effort," Bernice went on to say when Fanny seemed hesitant.

"I…I…I guess I could discuss it with her." Fanny finally managed to get the words out.

"All right," Bernice smiled for the first time during the conversation, "I'll tell her." And with that, she abruptly walked away, leaving Fanny standing there with a bundle of laundry and a head filled with a thousand thoughts of what she may have just gotten herself into.

43

Revelation

Something awful had happened to Mama. That much Audie knew; he just didn't understand exactly what it might have been. No one would talk to him about it. Not even Vera Reynolds, who was like a second mother to him, would discuss it with him. He felt frustrated.

And the way everyone in around here was acting! Miss Reynolds didn't want him or Robert to leave the yard. With summer going strong, there wasn't much fun to be had when you couldn't leave the yard. She wouldn't even allow them to go fishing!

All he did was help Mama pick up and deliver the washing. Yes, Mama was back to doing that job instead of going into Kingston. All the customers had weird looks on their faces when they saw Mama. It was like they were sorry for her and maybe a little scared. It was hard to read the faces of his neighbors. Mama was quieter than usual; besides that, Audie couldn't tell anything was wrong. But he knew *something was very wrong.*

Audie asked Robert if he knew what was going on with everyone. Robert answered, "Well, I'm not supposed to say anything about it to anyone…especially you."

Audie's brow was furrowed in frustration, "Robert, please…tell me!"

"I heard an old drunk attacked Miss Fanny when she walkin' home late one night. He…you know…" Robert didn't look Audie in the eye.

"What?!" Audie wanted to shout at his friend. "Please, just say it!"

"She was raped, Audie. Your mama was raped." Robert looked at his friend with empathy.

Audie's face was white. He had been sheltered from even talking about such heinous deeds, and he found it difficult to fathom the depth of depravity some folks sank into. He went from a feeling of incredulity to swift anger. He felt as though he could have killed this unknown man with his own bare hands at that very moment.

This became a turning point for Audie. It matured him in a way nothing else had or ever could. He vowed right then to never allow himself to be debased in that manner. He promised God he would always love and serve Him. He felt, maybe, the balance of good versus evil could be tilted for the good if he worked hard enough at making good on that vow.

44

A Time to Leave

Jane Anne was now almost two years old. A happy child she was, always smiling and laughing. She was very loving toward her older brother, whom she tried to follow everywhere. Vera Reynolds who babysat regularly, and especially her mother, Fanny, both loved the little girl immensely.

The child's face would light up as soon as her mother came into her sight. Jane's first words were *mama* and *Auie*. At first, she had some difficulty making the *d* sound. Now, she could vocalize her feelings quite well. She enjoyed going to church with her brother and sang the hymns throughout the week. Everyone listening to her couldn't help but smile.

She had red curly hair that wreathed a round, cherub-like face. Her eyes were a bright blue, and with her button nose and babyish expression, she appeared as a little red-haired angel. She was a source of pride for Fanny, and being her only girl child, she might have been a bit spoiled.

Audie did as much spoiling of his sister as did his mother. He loved Jane with the love only a brother can give. He was her protector, her teacher, and she was a source of joy to him.

Robert was a bit jealous of the attention Audie showed his little sister. If she wanted to tag along with the two of them, Audie was always happy to let her. Robert sometimes made an excuse to leave her behind just to be able to spend time with his friend without Jane about. Audie could tell it bothered Robert always having Jane around, and he understood that Robert had no, so it was an adjustment for him.

"Do you think your mom will ever have any more kids?" Audie asked Robert one day when the two of them went hiking up the mountain side.

"I dunno," Robert answered, "I don't think my dad wants any more kids."

"How come?"

"He said somethin' one time that he was sad he missed the years he didn't know I was around. He said he wanted to give me lots of attention, and if there are more kids around, he would have to divide the attention among the others. Thing is," Robert talked slowly, like he was thinking hard about what he was saying, "he never gave me that much attention anyways. Seems like all he did was work."

"I know. Momma was working a lot before…well, you know what happened." Audie didn't like talking about that subject. Wrapping his mind around the details had done something to him, and he didn't like the person he was since that revelation.

"Did ya ever want a brother or a sister?" Audie asked Robert.

"I guess," Robert shrugged his shoulders. "Do you like havin' a sister? I mean...I can tell you do."

"It's not whether I like having her or not," Audie explained. "She's here, and I just love her. I don't remember wanting her or not wanting her. But she is here, and that's all I care about."

"Yeah, I guess you're right," Robert said. "I never thought about it that way."

"Just like when you met your dad the first time. You didn't say to your mom, 'I want a dad or I don't want a dad,' he just showed up, and now, you have a dad. You love your dad, right?"

"Sure," Robert said. "I just wish he could spend more time with me." Robert stared down at his feet while he said this.

Audie was quiet and thoughtful, and then he said, "Maybe it's time you went back home, Robert. If you miss your dad, go home and tell him, 'cause maybe he don't know you want to spend time with him. Even if he would or could, he can't 'cause you're here. "

Robert looked up at Audie and said, "I think you're right."

So Audie knew that his friend would go back home soon, but that was all right. He felt like he had helped him figure out some things in his heart and mind, and now his friend needed to start over with his mom and dad in New York.

"You're a good friend, Audie."

"Ah," Audie said sheepishly, smiling, "so are you."

The boys ambled slowly back to the Reynolds's home, not talking.

45

All Things for Our Good

"Momma?"

"What, Audie?"

The two were seated at the old kitchen table in the one-roomed house her father had built. Jane sat in a high chair Ollie had given her. They were eating a supper of scrambled eggs and toast, a good cheap meal.

"Will you come with me to church this Sunday?"

Fanny looked at her son. He was growing up so fast. He was nearly as tall as she was. Right now, his eyes pleaded with her not to say no.

"Sweetheart, we've been through this before." She looked away from his gaze as she said this.

"But, Momma, I thought you would want to go…to thank God…for…well, you know." Now Audie was the one that looked away.

"Where did you hear something about what I should be thanking God for?" Fanny asked, sudden anger coming over her at the thought of anyone having the nerve to speak to her son about the rape.

"It…It was Robert. But don't be mad at him, Momma, please," he pleaded his cause to his mother on his friend's behalf. "I asked him if he knew anything about it. I wanted to know."

"Oh." Fanny didn't know what to say. She hadn't realized Robert was grown up enough to understand what had happened to her.

"He explained everything to me, and now I know. I'm glad I know, Momma. It helped me understand not just what happened to you but about all people."

She looked again at her son's young eyes. She noticed, for the first time, a maturity there she hadn't saw before. She saw that her little boy was becoming a man, and it brought tears to her eyes and a lump to her throat.

"Don't cry, Momma," he said, and he stood, walked around the table to her, and hugged her tightly.

Jane began to cry, wanting to be hugged also.

"I don't want you to be sad anymore. I want you to be happy again," he said, laying his head on her shoulder.

"I am happy, honey," She lifted his head, smiling through her tears. "How could I be sad with a son as wonderful as you?"

"Please, will you come to church on Sunday?" he asked, hopefully.

"I can't. Not yet, Audie. But one day, I'm sure I will." She offered this statement up truthfully.

Audie seemed to accept it. He knew that God was working inside his mother and that his time wasn't like our time. He knew his mother would one day come to church with him. That's the hope he held on to.

"Well, now," Fanny said, "let's get the supper dishes done and get ready for bed."

------◆------◆------

The days passed quickly, and September was upon them. Fanny's days did not vary much in the daily routine. It was picking up laundry, washing and drying it; the last order of business was the ironing of it, day after day.

She had gotten past the bone weariness of monotony. In fact, she found comfort in the familiar. That seems to be the pattern for most folks. Not unlike the serenity prayer, you gain the courage to accept those things you cannot change, and what isn't said, you learn to live with them.

Fanny certainly could not change what had happened to her, no matter how she might wish that she could. She learned to live with it. As time passed, she was able to sleep through the night without nightmares. She found she no longer needed to see Audie and Jane every moment of the day, and she didn't worry about their safety nonstop any longer.

There was really only one thing that bothered her now. She realized she had just missed her second "womanly visitor." She had been very nervous about the upcoming catering for the Barne's wedding reception. Perhaps it was stress-related. She'd been staving off a cold for about two weeks also. Could that have something to do with it?

As unsettling as it was, she made it a priority to think of other things. Things that kept her busy and productive. She recently had started potty training Jane. That became a large focus for her. It was little more than a week into that task that it seemed Jane had fully mastered the understanding of it.

Finally, unable to ignore the possibility of what it really could mean, Fanny approached Vera. She told her about her cycles and about what she feared could have happened. There was only one way to know for sure, Vera said.

An appointment with the doctor over in Kingston. Fanny said she couldn't go alone, she wouldn't.

"You don't have to. Ollie is coming the end of the month to get Robert. She'll go with you. I'll take care of the children."

"Robert is leaving you?" Fanny asked in surprise, temporarily forgetting her own problem.

"Yes, but it's a good thing. He figured out a few things while he was here, with Audie's help. I think he'll be much happier this time around. Of course, I'll miss him like crazy. That's why I'm so thankful I can help you with your kids," Vera smiled at Fanny.

"You've been just wonderful, Vera. I don't know what I'd have done without you throughout all of this," Fanny said, placing her hand over Vera's.

"Okay then. Let's make that appointment then."

◆———◆

The month went slower than time had ever gone for Fanny. She was so anxious to know whether she was pregnant she could barely stand it. Ollie arrived on schedule. If only she hadn't this problem, she might have really enjoyed having her here.

The best part of Ollie being here was that she could assist her with the wedding reception. That was an answer to prayer. She was a little amazed that God was listening to her prayers. She had thought He had given up on her.

Finally, the day of the doctor's appointment arrived. Ollie tried to keep her spirits lifted by telling her jokes and making her laugh. Ollie was always good for cheering her up, she thought to herself.

Once in the doctor's examining room, Fanny laid on the cold table, covered only by a sheet. With her feet in stirrups, she felt like she was on display for all the world to see. She was so embarrassed she covered her face with part of the sheet. Thank goodness there was a nurse in attendance. It helped to have another female present while the doctor's gloved hands probed her in ways she had never experienced, not even in the brothel.

Only a moment later, the doctor helped Fanny into a sitting position. He took off his gloves and said, "Yes, ma'am."

"What?" Fanny asked fearfully.

"Yes, you are pregnant."

46

Starting to Heal

The doctor assured Fanny nothing was amiss with her physically. She was healthy and about eight to nine weeks along. He suggested follow-ups for her prenatal care. He wrote out a prescription for some high-potency vitamins to keep her and the expected child well throughout the pregnancy.

Fanny listened. She heard what he said, but his voice seemed distant, as though she was hearing it over a long distance. The walk back home with Ollie beside her was silent. Ollie had linked her arm through hers, and the two walked. It was one of those rare occasions when Ollie did not know what she should say.

When they reached the Holden River Bridge, Fanny stopped. She stared at the bridge and then she tentatively stepped forward to cross it. Although the sun was shining, Fanny could not help but remember the dark night she had crossed this bridge in this same direction. The foot of the bridge was looming within mere steps. The fear and the anxiety she thought she had put to rest came flooding over her, and she could only sit down where she stood and cried. She cried as though she was a well from which the tears kept flowing, seemingly endless. With the tears came the washing away of an evil presence. In its place was the peace of God, which passes all human understanding. Ollie had sat quietly next to her, arm around her friend. She finally spoke as Fanny's sobbing subsided.

"Fan, don't look at this like a bad thing. Look at it as God is using the bad thing to give you something good. Like the Bible says, 'What the enemy meant for evil, God used for my good.' I know it's easy for me to say, but I really believe it's true," she spoke these words in a low, soothing voice.

Fanny looked at Ollie now, for the first time since they began the walk home. It was like it was the first time she was seeing her; a part of Fanny's mind wondered where Ollie had come from all of a sudden.

"Do you really think so?" Fanny's eyes, still wet with her tears, scanned Ollie's face, desperate to see something there, something that said hope.

"I really do." She managed a slight smile.

"I want to believe that," Fanny said, hugging her knees to her chest. "I really want to believe that."

"It's true," Ollie said.

Fanny threw all of her energy into getting everything ready for the wedding reception of Timothy and Elizabeth. She considered renting the equipment she needed but realized that if she wanted to continue the catering for other events, she would need something she could use on a regular basis.

Once she made those decisions, she set about making a list of the items she would need to make all the food. Ollie assisted by doing most of the leg work, the picking-up equipment, the going-to-get-the-food items, etc. Fanny would do all the cooking, Ollie would do the serving. They both did set up.

Fanny dressed in her hotel uniform. Ollie wore a long dark skirt and white blouse. The hall was decorated beautifully. The tables were covered with white linen; the stemmed glassware punctuated each setting with maroon napkins skillfully placed in each glass, flared to look like a fan. Centerpieces were lilies in crystal cut vases with a trail of baby roses cascading out of each base onto the white linen. In all, it was as elaborate a gathering Portage Bend had ever hosted.

The band played the standard favorites, and everyone danced. The bride and groom made their entrance, and all eyes were upon them. Both beamed like celebrities at an award ceremony. Vera had outdone herself on the wedding gown. Elizabeth really did look stunning.

Fanny watched the couple through a small crack in the doorway between hall and kitchen. She couldn't help but shed some tears as she saw Timothy with his new bride. He really seemed very happy. She was glad she felt enough magnanimity to be happy for him. She turned away and turned her attention back to the food.

Ollie came in, stating more chicken and potatoes were needed. She pulled out already prepared pans to refill the chafing dishes with. She could hear the music swell and someone made a toast to the happy couple. There was laughter and handclapping as Ollie carried first one pan and returned for the other.

Fanny opened the oven to check on the still cooking chicken. When she stood and turned around, Timothy was there in front of her, smiling. She froze, not knowing whether to turn her back to him or acknowledge his presence.

What seemed like hours but was only seconds, she managed to say, "What do you want?" her eyes carefully avoiding his.

"I wanted to see you and to thank you," he said, extending his hand to her.

"For what?" she asked.

"For being so sweet to agree to do this for Elizabeth and me. I wouldn't have been surprised if you had refused."

"It's nothing," she answered, still not looking directly at him. "I wanted the job." Meaning, "I wanted the money."

"Well, whatever the reason, I just wanted to say thank you," he said.

"You're welcome," she said and glanced at his face.

She saw the same look she remembered so well. A mixture of sweetness and boyishness, like a child in the man's body. She looked away quickly. She couldn't help but see how much Jane looked like her father.

"I have to go," he said, and he turned and walked through the door, back to his wife.

Fanny gripped the kitchen counter, her heart aching. No, she would not allow him to have control over her emotions again. She stood up straighter and held her chin higher. She might be many things, but she was not a quitter. She would finish this job, and she would do it well. No one would ever be able to say anything less about Fanny Small.

47

A Second Blessing

With her earnings from the wedding reception, Fanny bought some things for the baby she was now expecting. Things she would never have thought about if she hadn't earned this money. Like baby bottles and new diapers; premade ones, not dirty old rags turned into diapers. She felt as though it made the pregnancy seem legitimate. It didn't matter how this life inside of her got started, it was a life, and Fanny was determined she would give this child the best shot at having a good life that she possibly could.

She didn't want to make it obvious to the rest of the world she was pregnant. So just as she had done before Jane was born, she watched what she ate, and, of course, she always got plenty of exercise. No one need know until the child was born. She didn't want the pity or the judgment of anyone.

With Vera's help, she sewed together small gowns in neutral colors since she didn't know whether the child was girl or boy. She still had Jane's baby clothes in the event she had another girl. God had certainly answered her prayer as a young girl when she told Him she wanted to be a mother one day. She would have never dreamed all her children would have different fathers. She used to think she'd be a lucky girl if one man on this earth wanted to be with her that way. Having grown up knowing she wasn't pretty had made her believe her chances of being with a man were slim. Still, she had thought she'd be a married woman one day, certainly by the time she had three children. Funny how life works things out, she thought wistfully.

Audie was a product of her job choice at an early and innocent age. She had loved Timothy and willingly gave herself to him; Jane was the result of that love. Now she was having her third child because a wicked, selfish, and drunken man had taken what she would not have given him under any other circumstance. Were any of them less precious to her because of the way each was conceived? No, not by any means. She loved both of her children and would die for them, if necessary. When this little one would be born, Fanny would love and cherish him or her equally.

Even now, she looked upon her belly, thinking how helpless and miraculous a child in utero truly was. Knit together by the creator, known to Him in ways she could not fathom, she marveled at the awesome responsibility that motherhood had bestowed upon her. She knew when she felt the first stirring of that life that she would never do anything as important as being this child's mother. Many women have babies. Only love can make that woman a mother.

The winter months came and went. Now, spring was imminent. Fanny was in her third trimester. She had seen the obstetrician in Kingston only one more time since the initial examination. She explained to him she couldn't afford to come every month. She also told him she had bore her first two children at home and she would do the same with this one. Although he was not approving of her attitude, he consented since she was strong and healthy. If nothing unexpected came about, she shouldn't have any problems giving birth at home again.

At the beginning of March that year, Fanny began living with Vera. This seemed the wisest course of action as her due date came closer. She moved slower these days, gathering up the neighbor's laundry and dutifully doing the work she needed to do to earn a wage. Vera pleaded with her to stop working so hard. At least, cut back a few days so she could rest.

Fanny reluctantly agreed to give up two days a week. Whether she wanted to admit it to herself or not, it was evident she was having a hard time of it. Her back ached constantly. Her feet and ankles were swelling, so she could barely walk in a pair of shoes. She was so tired all the time. Vera was worried about her.

Vera could tell that things with this pregnancy were different. Granted, Fanny had fulfilled her job duties during the entire nine months carrying Jane until she delivered. She had been fine throughout that pregnancy. This time that was not the case.

So it was that when Fanny began having contractions, Vera sent Audie for the only nurse in Porter's Bend, Bernice McField. When she arrived, she was businesslike in her take charge attitude. She seemed only a little surprised to find out Fanny was with child and was now in her ninth month, ready to give birth.

Bernice's nursing training was evident as she bustled about, confident and cool. She told Audie to stay out of the room with his little sister. Reluctant to leave his mother's side, he did what he was told.

In what was a very short labor, Fanny brought forth a second son. Exhausted, she slept while the infant wailed his first cries. Bernice cleaned him up and wrapped him up tight in a blanket and handed him over to Vera. She left the home with Fanny still asleep and Vera calling out a hasty thank you.

Vera laid the child in a dresser drawer lined with warm sheets while she made a mixture of cow's milk and corn syrup. Then she fed the little boy, allowing his mother to get some sleep. She wondered to herself what name Fanny might have chosen for this second son.

48

Going Home

Vera Reynolds awoke to a baby's cry; she glanced at the clock that said 3:25 a.m. She went to check Fanny before she looked in on the baby. Fanny still slept, her face white, her chest scarcely moving with the breath from her lungs. Vera felt for a pulse. Weak, but it was there. She prayed fervently for Fanny's return to health. What would happen if she never woke up and just drifted away into death? What would these children do? She loved them like her own but felt she was too old to start raising kids all over again.

She turned her attention to the baby. He was red from exerting all his energy crying, trying to eat his own little fists. She changed his diaper and warmed a bottle for him. As she sat with him, rocking and feeding him, she looked at Fanny, sleeping. Her heart ached for her. She had suffered so much in her young life already. When the baby was fed, she put him back in his makeshift bed. She heard a rustling and turned to see Fanny, thrashing about. Her eyes were open.

"Fanny?" she said.

"Where am I," Fanny asked as she looked around the room wildly.

"You're with me, Vera. You just had a baby boy, remember?" she asked her gently, probing.

"Vera? Why can't I remember?"

"You've been under a lot of stress, sweetie, that's all."

"I have a baby boy?"

"Yes, you do. See." Vera picked the child up and held him close to Fanny's face so she could see him.

"Oh…" She reached for him and held him. Fanny was becoming more alert and wakeful when Vera posed the question.

"Do you have a name in mind?"

"I was thinking of calling him Tobias after Uncle George's father. What do you think?" She managed to remember the name she'd been deciding on for her new son. She looked at her newborn and when she looked at Vera, her eyes seemed uncertain it was the right name for him.

"I mean, we could call him Toby for short. That sounds more like a little boy's name."

"I like it," Vera said, smiling. "What about a middle name?"

"Would it be wrong…," Fanny paused, looking down, "if I gave him 'Timothy' for his middle name?"

"It's a name. Why not?" Vera said, pretending not to know why Fanny asked her about its being right or wrong.

"Then that's his name. Tobias Timothy Small."

Fanny was pleased with the sound of it. It was a good strong name for a good strong man.

✦———✦

Within two weeks of Toby's birth, Fanny was feeling more like her old self. The little boy grew quickly; he seemed to gain weight just by breathing. By the end of his first month, he smiled. Fanny had never known a baby so young to smile. Vera laughed and told her it was surely gas.

No, Fanny insisted. Toby seemed to know that she was the mother. His eyes fastened on her, and anything she uttered made him smile. It was nice to see he was a happy little boy, considering the way he had been conceived.

Audie was a big help too. He would diaper him, feed him, talk to him. Jane, on the other hand, was displaced as the baby of the family and let everyone know how upset that made her. She stomped around, crying, and even threw herself headlong on the hard floor, which really made her cry. She was the only one who seemed upset about having a baby in the house. Fanny knew it would take time for her to adjust to having a little brother and just allowed her to have her little tantrums. She would learn that this kind of acting out was not going to get her any more attention.

It was time, Fanny knew, to go back home to the one-room house. Vera had been extraordinarily generous to her, but she needed to be independent. So the four of them packed up and went back home.

When she had settled in the first night, she looked around. Audie was studying. Jane was playing with her doll. Toby was sound asleep. Fanny felt a contentment she hadn't felt in a very long time. Why it happened now, she wasn't sure. She only knew that God had protected her all these years and blessed her with three beautiful children. She felt humbled at the thought of all He had done for her.

"Audie?" she said to her son.

"Yes, Momma?" he answered her.

"How would you like to take me with you to church this Sunday?"

Audie's face broke into a wide grin, and jumping up, he ran to his mother's side and hugged her so hard she thought her ribs would break. She laughed. He laughed too. They kept laughing until tears rolled down their cheeks.

"I love you, Momma," Audie whispered into her ear.

"I love you just as much right back," she whispered to him in return.

What could life do to her now? Nothing could be sweeter than this, right now, this moment.

49

The Mission Field

It was late April, 1917. World War I was in its third year. Fanny was trying desperately to put all her faith in God and not be anxious over her son's missionary trip. It was the hardest thing she would ever attempt to do.

That Sunday in church, Audie's appointment was announced. He would be going to El Salvador to work alongside seasoned missionaries who would train him until he was capable of working on his own. Fanny was glad Audie wasn't going where there was fighting going on. That she knew of. It was the unknown that was frightening.

It was determined that he would leave May 6. Audie began to prepare his departure with fervent prayer for God's guidance. He didn't know what dangers he would face when he got there, but he wanted God to know he would be ready no matter what.

He was going to go by train to Florida. From there, he would board a plane to El Salvador. The prospect of taking either mode of transportation was exciting all by itself, but the real thrill was knowing he was doing the work of God. What could be better in life than this?

❖————❖

On the day Audie left, Fanny couldn't help but feel as though her son had died. Her heart was near bursting with pride; it was just that he would be so far away. She could not have been more saddened than if he actually had been lying in a coffin rather than getting on the train at the Kingston depot. He waved good-bye to his mother, brother, and sister until they were no longer visible. Fanny stood on the platform, straining her eyes to see the tiny spot in the distance.

"Maw, can we go now?" Toby whined impatiently.

"Don't talk like that to Momma. Can't you see how distraught she is?" Jane enjoyed using words that Toby didn't understand. She had always excelled in vocabulary, and it was fun to flaunt it with her less educated brother.

"Aw, don't throw yer big words around," Toby taunted her. "Yer ain't so smart."

"I'm smarter than you'll ever be," Jane replied, tossing her head to emphasize her point.

"Hush, you two. Can we please have some peace and quiet?" Fanny begged of them.

"I'm sorry, Momma," Jane said. Toby said nothing, just walked along with them, hands stuffed in his pockets.

The trio walked back home, across the bridge, and then to the house. Fanny fell into a chair, feeling utterly exhausted, both emotionally and physically.

"Momma," Jane asked, "would you like me to make some tea for you?"

Fanny looked up at her daughter, so eager to please, so sweet.

"Yes, that would be nice. Thank you. "

Jane smiled happily and hurried to make the tea.

Toby headed for the door once again, thinking his mother's attention had been diverted.

"Where are you going, Toby?"

He stopped and turned around, looking at his mother. "Maw, I hope you ain't plannin' on me hangin' 'round here all the time just 'cause Audie's gone."

"No, I don't," Fanny said sharply in return to her son's insolent remark. "I do expect you to tell me where you're going and when you plan to be back. This is still my house, and you're not yet a man. You'll do as I say…or else."

"Else, what?" Toby looked her straight in the eye, defiantly.

Fanny merely sighed and looked away. She felt so weak when it came to disciplining Toby.

Toby chuckled to himself as he strode out the door.

The plane that carried Audie into the city of San Salvador was small; only twelve passengers were aboard. The ride in had been bumpy; some turbulence had left Audie feeling shaken up.

At the small airport, he met Juan. Juan was an American citizen originally from the area of San Salvador. His family had moved to America just after he was born. He had become a Christian as a child. He had harbored the desire to return to El Salvador and preach the gospel. He and his wife had done just that.

Juan was about forty years of age. Along with his wife, his two children were there with him. He had a small contraption that resembled a golf cart to transport Audie and his belongings to their house. Audie would be staying with them until he could manage a place of his own.

Audie had tried to learn about El Salvador before he left, but nothing prepared him for the poverty he witnessed on the way to Juan's house. Barefoot, barely clad children approached them, begging for change. Old men laid on the roadsides, covered with their own feces and flies. Ramshackle huts, if they could even be called that, dotted muddy streets in the sections of the city Juan traveled through. The eyes of the mothers and the children, so filled with desperation and hopelessness, haunted him.

Juan's house was separate from the hovels; it set apart by itself on about one half acre. It was fashioned from stucco, a large flat-roofed house all on one level. Inside, it was very clean. Juan's wife, Maria, was introduced to Audie. He politely shook her hand. Juan's daughter and son were teenagers. They were both very serious and polite.

Audie's room was spacious, with a twin bed covered with a light bedspread. A window overlooked the family vegetable garden. An adjoining room was used for a bathroom. There was a pump and a washbasin. No tub or sink. Audie remembered thinking to himself, "I thought I grew up poor. This is much worse." In reality, Audie had not realized the extent of the country's poverty. Little did he know it, but the poor people of San Salvador considered Juan's family to be rich folks. And indeed, they were.

Most of the shacks had no running water. The people had to walk two miles to a small stream to get water for drinking and bathing. Often the water was muddy and was unfit for consumption. Illness such as dysentery was rampant. There were no bathrooms. People defecated wherever they happened to be. The smell amidst the shacks was sickening.

Once Audie settled in, Juan spoke to him. He explained the plight of the poor people and what they were trying to do for them. First, they tried to alleviate their suffering with clean water, which the churches in America sent in gallon jugs. Juan and his family would then distribute them throughout the poor sections of the village along with staples like foods and clothing. They had built a clinic inside the business section to care for the sick people who couldn't afford traditional doctors. Next, they shared their faith with the people and encouraged them to accept Jesus. Even though they were poor and suffering, once they accepted Jesus and understood His sacrifice for them, they knew true joy.

They had built an open air church where many locals came and rejoiced in their salvation. It was joyous to see the people who, even though horribly impoverished, would dance to the altar and lay a small coin down as an offering to God. They were so happy to give back whatever they had, and they did so with a glad heart.

He prepared Audie physically and mentally with all he would be faced with when going out to minister to the local people. Juan wanted him to know how difficult it was going to be.

After they discussed these things, Juan took Audie with him to one of the shacks that belonged to a family who had recently been converted to Christianity. They took some water and other things the family could use with them. Upon entering the hovel, Audie could not help but be struck with the smiles of the mother and father and children. There was nothing in the shack except cardboard slabs, which each family member used as a bed. They had to sit on the dirt floor. Audie felt a lump rise up in his throat as the father told him how he came to know Jesus in broken English. He had never imagined anyone could live as these people had to live.

As they traveled the road back to Juan's house, Audie could no longer contain himself but cried for the plight of these good, poor people. Juan let him cry until he could cry no more. He told him it was good to see that Audie was truly a compassionate human being and had a tender heart for the Lord.

50

Joy and Trials

Jane was missing her brother Audie something awful. He always read from the Bible to them after supper. The house was painfully quiet without his voice reciting the Psalms or some other Bible passage. His bed was made and empty. She knew he was doing what he was born to do, but it didn't make her heart ache any less for him.

She knew her mother was suffering equally. Together, the two of them were miserable company for one another. Her mother sat, mending socks Toby had worn holes into. She methodically threaded her needle and thread through the socks, but she could tell her mind was not on the mending. Jane couldn't help but notice the small lines beginning to form around her mother's eyes. Lines that bespoke hard work and anxiety.

Jane so wished Toby would get his act together. He didn't seem to care if Momma worried herself to death over him. As if Audie being half a world away wasn't enough for her to bear. Talking to Toby was a lost cause. He wouldn't listen to anyone, and he respected no one. She wasn't sure he even knew how to respect himself. She sighed, thinking about it all.

The only thing she could do was write a letter to Audie. He always knew the right things to say to make her feel better. Not that she would want to worry him. She would just ask him what to do if there was a hypothetical situation; he didn't have to know it was Toby, although she figured he would realize that it was. But, still, she felt the need to communicate with him. At least she could talk to him, even if she had to wait to hear an answer.

She set about finding her notebook and a pen to write with. Fanny asked her what she was doing, saying she thought Jane had finished her schoolwork for the evening.

"Yes, I did, Momma," she said. "I thought I'd write to Audie, you know, just to say hi."

"What a wonderful idea," her mother replied, wondering to herself what Audie was doing at that very moment.

"Tell him I said hello and that I love him," she instructed Jane. "I'll write a letter to him also, tomorrow."

"I know he is probably missing us just terribly," Jane said, and having said it out loud, she burst into tears. "I'm sorry, Momma," she said between sobs, "I just miss him so much!"

"I know, child. So do I," her mother said, not looking up from her mending.

Jane dried her eyes on her dress sleeve and said, "I know, Momma," and she began her letter to her brother,

"Dear Audie..."

Many weeks and letters between Audie and his family passed. Weeks gave way to years. Soon, Jane was graduated from eighth grade. Toby was now nearly thirteen and stood a head taller than his mother.

Fanny had planned a small party in honor of the graduation at Vera's house. She made a chocolate cake, and they had store-bought ice cream for the occasion. She had used half of her saved money for a necklace made of gold filigree with a locket on it. Inside, she had placed a picture of Audie. She was sure that Jane would love it.

A few of Jane's friends had been invited as well. Since parties of any sort were rare, it was something none of them would forget. Everyone ate cake and ice cream until they fairly burst, and the guest of honor cried when she opened her mother's present.

"Oh, Momma! It must have cost a fortune!"

"Not nearly what you are worth, my dear," Fanny said, smiling at her daughter. *So grown up now*, she thought.

"What are your plans now, Jane?" Vera asked Jane.

Jane shrugged her shoulders, saying, "I'm really not sure, but I'd really love to continue my education and maybe be a teacher." The hopefulness in her voice broke Fanny's heart because she knew it would take a miracle from God to make that happen.

Toby stood in the background of the group, leaning against the wall, arms folded across his massive chest. He cleared his throat loudly. The group hushed, and all eyes turned to him.

"Jane's got a boyfriend. She's prob'ly gonna run off with him, if she don't get knocked up first," he made this statement and stood there with a malicious grin on his face.

Vera was heard to take in a sharp breath. Jane's friends were too astounded to say anything.

Fanny said to Toby through clenched teeth, "Apologize to your sister for saying such a crude, awful lie!"

"I ain't gonna. It's true, and she knows it," he replied with his usual defiance.

Fanny looked at her daughter, whose head hung in embarrassment and shame. Her face was beet red, and her eyes were watery as she fought to hold back her tears.

Jane looked at her brother and said with shaking voice, "Thanks, Toby, for ruining an otherwise wonderful day!" Then she pushed her way past everyone and ran out the front door of the Reynolds's home. Fanny turned to follow her, but Vera held on to her arm to stop her.

"Let her go. She needs to be alone for now,"

Toby laughed loudly and left through the back doorway.

"Okay, everyone, the party is over," Fanny said, and the friends of Jane's she had invited left one by one, thanking Fanny and Vera for having them. Each of them looked shell shocked by Toby's behavior.

"Where did I go wrong with him?" Fanny asked Vera in exasperation.

"I don't think you had anything to do with it at all," Vera said. And that wisdom would sustain Fanny through the many years ahead.

Audie's life of missionary work began to take on a somewhat routine daily shape. He rose each day, said his prayers, and read his Bible, cleaned himself up, ate a scant breakfast, and went to one or more of the shacks in the poverty-riddled streets of San Salvador.

He would see first some of the people who had already accepted Jesus as their Savior. He encouraged them through the word and with basic necessities. Then he broadened his witnessing of God to the unchurched and lost. He also provided them with basic necessities, showing the love of Christ, which, in turn, would be incentive to bring them to the Savior by these acts of love.

This took up a large part of Audie's days. Then he would go to the clinic the church operated and assist with whatever they needed. Sometimes he would help transport those who needed it; other times he would counsel the parents or children of sick family members, showing them someone did care for them.

Finally, late into the evening, he would return to Juan and Maria's home, pray, and read his Bible and fall into bed for a few hours sleep and do it all over again the next day. He was exhausted but fulfilled.

The way Audie saw it, if God never did anything for him ever again, he would continue to do this every day the rest of his life, and he would still owe a debt he would never be able to repay. Such was his great love for his God.

51

Toby

Toby was not one to waste his time in school. He had some friends whose mothers made them go. One of them had told him about a bunch of girls that included his sister, Jane, talking about how dreamy the new assistant teacher was.

Of course, he could use this information to humiliate her when the opportunity presented itself. Graduation was coming soon, and that would be a good time to spring something on her, he thought craftily. If Maw was worried over Jane getting tangled up with some fellow, she wouldn't be looking at *him* quite so much.

Now Toby had let the cat out of the bag about Jane having a beau. Jane was worried Momma might wonder if it was really true. She tried to conjure up something to say if Momma asked her about it. He wasn't *exactly* a boyfriend—at least, not yet. She did like him though. He was so tall, and she thought him handsome, with a kind of Lincoln-esque quality about him—without the beard.

Nathan McConnel Scott was the assistant teacher sent to help the main teacher in Porter's Bend. Jane couldn't help but be smitten with his lanky frame, a mop of dark hair that fell across his forehead and into his sky-blue eyes. He had a nice smile too, she thought to herself the first day he appeared in their classroom. In spite of his height, he seemed shy when Mr. Carter introduced him as the assistant teacher. Jane found this quality charming.

When Jane and Momma, attended the midweek service at church, Nathan was there. She kept glancing his way during the hymn singing. He certainly seemed to put his heart into it, she noticed. It was gratifying to her to see he was a good Christian man. Even Momma could not find fault with him because of that, she pondered to herself happily.

After the service, she approached him. "Good evening, Mr. Scott. I'm Jane Small, one of the students at the school." She smiled, hoping he might remember her from the classroom.

"Oh, of course. How are you?" he scanned her face as he probed his brain to remember this girl among the sea of faces from the hours prior.

"Could I introduce you to my mother?" She lifted her hand toward Fanny, who stood with a group of ladies, discussing the weather or some such thing.

"Certainly," he replied and walked with Jane to the group of ladies.

"Momma," she said tentatively, "this is Mr. Scott. He's the new assistant teacher at school. He just started recently."

Fanny took the proffered hand Nathan held out to her and shook it. She couldn't help but see the look on her daughter's face, which foretold of a crush on the man.

"Hello," Fanny said politely. "Are you from around these parts?" she questioned him.

"No, actually," he told them, "I'm from Alabama, born and bred. My grandparents came over from Ireland and settled there some time ago."

"Oh, I see," Fanny said with interest. She tried to judge Nathan Scott's age from his face. She figured him to be somewhere between nineteen to twenty-five years of age. Too old for Jane, she thought.

"I've never been to Alabama. What's it like?" Jane wondered aloud. She seemed overly enthusiastic in everything she said to him.

Fanny thought she certainly must have a talk with her daughter about the proper way to conduct herself with a man.

"Well, it gets pretty hot there in the summers. The good part is that it doesn't get too cold in the winter. It's real pretty country down there. You should visit sometime," he recommended as he summed up his appraisal of his home state.

"Oh, I'd love to!" Jane said, her heart written all over her face.

"Well, it was really nice meeting you," Fanny said, "but we have to be going, now." She led her daughter away while

Jane kept looking back over her shoulder at Nathan Scott, calling out as Fanny led her away,

"I'll see you in class tomorrow, Mr. Scott!"

Once outside the church house, Fanny chuckles to herself.

"What's so funny, Momma?"

"You!"

"Why am I funny?"

"Jane Anne Small, don't you know how obvious you are being with that man? He is handsome, I know, but play a little hard to get. You don't want him thinking you're a floozy or something..."

"Momma! A floozy! I was just being nice to him!" Jane's hackles began to rise as she listened to her mother's comments.

"Janie, honey, face it. You have limited experience with men. I'm telling you, you were very obviously attracted to him. If I could see it, so could he."

"Oh no! I don't want him to think badly of me, Momma!" Jane wailed.

"It's all right! Don't take on so! Just, next time you see him, don't gush so much! Be discreet."

"Yes, I can do that!" Relieved, Jane was happy once again.

52

Turning Point

It had been two years since Audie left Porter's Bend for El Salvador. Jane was now sixteen years old. Toby was soon going to have his fifteenth birthday. As her children grew into adulthood, Fanny couldn't help but remember the time when they were infants and then toddlers with a warm nostalgia.

If only they could stay small and innocent like that forever, she thought wistfully. Of course, that was not why mothers had children. They were never really mine, she realized. I was just being lent them for a time. During that time, she was expected to raise them and give them the values God wanted them to have. She hoped that she had done what He wanted with these children. She believed in her heart that she had.

Nathan Scott had begun formally calling on Jane. He announced his intentions to Fanny that Sunday after church service when he asked to walk Jane home. Fanny knew he was a good, kind, Christian man who would treat her daughter well and would most certainly make good on the courtship culminating in marriage. She envied her daughter that in some respects, although she fought the feeling, knowing she shouldn't be jealous of her own daughter. God had His reasons for why her life had taken the roads she had traveled.

Toby had taken to hanging out with girls who possessed a certain reputation. Cheap and unchurched, she had told him. These kinds of girls would not bring him any satisfaction, at least, not in the long run. He turned a deaf ear to all she had to say in the matter.

Fanny supposed it was typical male behavior for a boy to sow his wild oats, but she had gotten so accustomed to Audie. He was all about loving and serving the Lord, so it was difficult to go through this with Toby.

Toby kept company with a few girls, but one in particular, Lucy Dowdy, was the one he saw the most. Lucy would have been a pretty girl if she had tried. Being born dirt poor, Lucy didn't have nice clothes or money for luxuries. Her hair was long but dry from using the homemade lye soap to wash it. She was a typical poor white girl from the hills of Tennessee. Everyone thought Lucy's prospects were poor when it came to marriage. She had a reputation among the folks of Porter's Bend. Fanny didn't like knowing her son frequented being with Lucy.

However, she did see him trying to start a conversation with Sarah Brewster. Her father was a banker in Kingston; the mother was a stay-at-home mom. They had a nice, moderately priced home. Now, Sarah could be just what it would take to bring Toby into line, Fanny found herself thinking.

Sarah was beautiful, which Fanny realized was the main attraction for Toby. She was also sure her parents were going to throw barriers up to anything developing between their daughter and her son. Well, miracles still could happen. Fanny would pray over the situation.

As for Toby, it was true he really liked Sarah. She was so pretty with her long blond hair and vibrant blue eyes. She spoke softly, and even though she knew he was not what was considered a "good" fellow, she was never rude or stuck up with him. When she smiled at him, he felt an odd feeling in his chest. None of the so-called loose girls he had been with had given him such a feeling.

He walked with Sarah when the church services let out on Sunday evening. Mrs. Brewster took notice of her daughter and Toby conversing. "Sarah! Come here, please," she called out. She told him she had to go and went obediently to walk alongside her mother the rest of the way home. Toby stood there, watching her until he couldn't see her anymore. How was he ever going to be able to talk with her when her parents were always around, he thought to himself.

Undeterred, he wrote a note to Sarah, explaining to her how much he liked and admired her. Then he gave it, sealed in an envelope, to Nathan to give to Sarah before or after church services. He waited anxiously until then, to see what her response to the letter would be.

When all the folks began to come out the church door, Toby leaned on a tree trunk, out of sight, in case her parents might see him and drag Sarah away. There they were. When the two passed down the path to walk home, he waited for Sarah.

When he saw her, she was walking with another girl. Maybe if he approached her, she would talk with him and her friend would go on ahead. He debated this course of action for a moment and then stepped out.

He approached Sarah and her friend.

"Hey, Sarah," he said, as they were within speaking distance.

"Hey, Toby," Sarah replied, stopping. "Mary, you go on ahead. I'll just be a minute," she said to her friend, just as Toby had hoped.

"Toby, I can't talk long. My mother will be looking for me," she said this with concern in her eyes as she looked down the path, although her parents were now out of sight.

"I know," he said, "I just wondered...did Nate give you...my letter?" He felt embarrassed but didn't know why. It was hard for him to look in those beautiful eyes. His heart beat so fast.

"Yes. You are sweet to say such nice things about me," she said.

"Well, I wasn't trying to be sweet. It's all true." Now, he stole a quick look toward her face. She was smiling a little.

"Toby, don't be mad, but...your spelling is awful!"

Now, he was more embarrassed. "Well, I never was any good at school stuff." He looked down at his shoes, not sure what to say.

"It's not too late, you know. I could help you...if you wanted," she said softly.

"Really? What about your maw and paw?"

"Well, I would just say I was tutoring a student at school. That way, no one will be suspicious if I'm late getting home."

Toby was surprised by Sarah. She was coming up with this without his prompting. He realized she must like him as well. His face revealed his thoughts.

She laughed in reply.

"Okay, that'd be great," he agreed.

"I'll tell them I'm staying after school tomorrow then. Meet me in front of the school at 3:00 p.m."

"Don't school get out at 2:45?"

"I don't want the others to see us together."

He smiled back at her. She was positively devious. He loved it.

"All right."

"Listen, I *have* to go now," she said.

He nodded, understanding, as Sarah took off in a run to catch up with her friend.

He stood there, thinking about what just happened, amazed. Sarah Brewster. He could scarcely believe it! Then in a burst of gladness, he jumped up in the air and yelled, just for the sheer happiness of it. He was going to be spending time with Sarah Brewster!

◆——————◆

When Toby arrived at 3:00 p.m. at the school, he made his way up to the side yard, waiting. He didn't see anyone around, but he didn't want to make his presence known, just in case there was someone still inside.

Then, when he rounded the front of the building, walking slowly, he saw her sitting on the steps.

He walked up to her and sat next to her.

They just looked at each other for a long moment. Then, to Toby's amazement, Sarah leaned forward and kissed him.

He very much wanted to return the kiss, but something made him stop. He didn't want to mess this up. Sarah was a good girl. He didn't want to scare her.

"Wow. What was that?" he said softly, his heart beating like a drum within his chest.

"Didn't you like it?" she asked him coyly.

"Oh, yeah, it was...really nice," he told her. "It's just... I'm surprised, is all."

"You think I'm a goody-goody, don't you?"

"I think...I don't know...I...you tell *me*," Toby was faltering for the right words to say.

"I guess I am," she said. "But I don't want you to think of me that way. "

"Why not?" Toby asked her, in somewhat astonishment.

"Because I like you," she nudged him with her shoulder, smiling.

Toby couldn't believe he was sitting here with Sarah Brewster and she was telling him she liked him. She was so beautiful, he thought, looking at her. He felt slightly lightheaded.

"Really? You really do?" He knew he was repeating himself, but he didn't care.

"I do."

He felt like he could have stayed there, just like this, looking at her, forever. It was one of those moments he would never forget.

He mentally shook himself and finally broke the silence, "Do you want to take a walk?"

"Okay."

They walked together, around the school house, holding hands. They talked about everything. He talked about his mom, Audie, and Jane. How he wanted to see the world and never have to answer to anyone. She talked about her family, school, and getting married and having children some day. She did say she'd always gone to church and that it was an important part of her life. She didn't try to shove it down his throat, though, like others always did. He found that to be very kind of her.

When they parted that day, they made plans to meet on a day later in the week. Toby kissed her on the cheek before she started the walk home. This must be what Maw said respecting a girl was like. He knew he never would want to hurt her or scare her, and he felt an overwhelming desire to protect her. He knew, if called upon, he would gladly have died for her.

Yes, this must be what Maw meant. Respect and love. It really was a powerful combination.

        ❖━━━❖

Toby knew Sarah was the real deal because his desire to be with anyone else had totally evaporated. He loved and respected Sarah so much. In fact, he felt he could wait for as long as he needed to be with her intimately.

He found himself thinking about her constantly and looking forward to their "tutoring" sessions anxiously. Just to be around her was like heaven for him.

He found also that he wanted to give her nice gifts. But with no money, that was difficult. He decided he needed to find a job just so he could give her whatever her heart desired. She never asked for anything, which only made him want to give her things even more. He took on a job in Kingston at the granary, lifting bags of meal onto and off trucks.

No one was more surprised at this turn of events than Fanny. She was amazed to see her youngest son awake at the crack of dawn, washed up and dressed, and heading out the door.

"Where are you going so early?" she questioned him, the first day this happened.

"Got a job over in Kingston. Gotta be there by 7:00 a.m.," he said this so matter-of-factly, as though nothing was out of the ordinary.

Fanny was speechless at this news. She feared to say anything lest she jinx it.

But each weekday morning, he did the same thing. She was truly thankful to God that, finally, her little boy was coming around to his senses.

And with Sarah's heart as his only motivation, Toby worked with a zest he didn't know he possessed. After two weeks of working, he received his first paycheck. Elated, he went straight to the bank and cashed it. He would spend every cent on Sarah.

After Toby left the bank, he started for home. Along the way, he passed a jewelry store. He looked at the display of necklaces, rings, and such. Some of the price tags were four times the sum of his paycheck. Besides, he thought, it's probably too soon for something like that. Although, he would have given her a ring in a second had he thought she would accept it.

Walking on, he approached a pawn shop. There, in the window, was a music box. It was carved wood, with flowers and a violin on the sides and top. The lid was open, and a velvet cushion was visible, with a gold ribbon crossing over it. Toby went inside to investigate.

He asked the man behind the counter about the music box. He showed Toby how to wind it up with a key on the bottom of the box, and as long as the lid was open, it played "My Wild Irish Rose" in a lilting tinkling sort of way. The clerk told him he could have the box for ten dollars. Toby said he'd take it, and the man wrapped it up for him. He knew for a certainty that Sarah would love it.

He wasn't able to see Sarah for a couple of days. His anticipation of that was going to be hard to contain now, especially with this gift he wanted to give to her. Since he had started talking to Sarah, Toby noticed he felt happier. He didn't argue with his Maw as much and found no pleasure in tormenting his sister any longer. He didn't understand it, but he was happy about it just the same.

Fanny had noticed the changes taking place in her son also. Of course, there was the responsibility of taking on a job. She didn't know what else was going on in his life because Toby was not the sharing type, especially not with his mother.

When Toby came home that day, he entered the house smiling. Fanny said to him, "You seem to be in a good mood."

"I guess I am," he answered. He took a seat and removed the boots he had worn for the day's work.

"What's in the package, if I'm allowed to ask?"

"Well…" Toby looked at his mother. She looked as though she expected a smart retort from him, and a part of him thought about that. Then he took a breath and said, "Maw, I think I'm in love," he hesitated, waiting for her to laugh or something like that.

Fanny didn't laugh. She just said, "How do you know?"

Toby told his mother about Sarah. He surprised himself how good it felt to say it out loud to someone. At least, he knew his mother cared about him. She wasn't going to tell him he was crazy or something. He told her how he felt when he was near her, how he wanted to protect her and give her the world, if only he could.

Fanny smiled. "I guess you really are in love, son." It was so good to know she understood and was happy for him.

"Anyway, this is a present for her," Toby said, lifting the package onto the table. "It's a music box. It's real nice. I think she'll really like it."

"Oh, I'm sure she will, honey. It's just…," she hesitated, "how do her parents feel about you seeing their daughter?"

Toby stared at the floor. "They don't know about us."

He explained how Sarah had made up the story about tutoring a student in order to spend time with him. Fanny's brows rose in surprise. She hadn't thought Sarah would do something like that, but then *she* had told her share of lies at this age.

"When do you think you'll tell them?"

"Why do I hafta tell them?" Toby looked angry for a second, thinking of Sarah's parents trying to keep them apart.

"She's fourteen, for starters, and their only daughter. They should know, Toby."

"I can't let them take her away," Toby said, sounding scared. Fanny had never known Toby to be scared of anyone or anything.

"Son," she told him, "if it's meant to be, it will be. No matter what her parents may say or don't say. This is when you have to trust God and put your faith in Him."

Toby thoughtfully mulled over her words. He loved Sarah so much he just couldn't bear the thought of losing her. If trusting God was what it took to keep her in his life, maybe...he should think about doing that.

He made no reply to his mother's advice. He simply said, "I think I'll nap till supper. I'm really tired."

Fanny silently said a prayer for Toby as he went to lie across his bed. She hoped and prayed that God would not punish him for being so rambunctious most of his young life. This was an important turning point for Toby. She fervently prayed it would all work out.

53

Complications

After two years of courting Jane, Nathan Scott asked her to marry him. Naturally, she said yes. Fanny was pleased and proud but sad she couldn't give the couple much in the way of financial support. Nathan told Fanny not to worry about it; the couple wanted only a small ceremony in the Baptist Church.

A June wedding was planned and executed. The happy couple went to Alabama on their honeymoon to meet Nathan's parents and possibly to find a place there to settle. Fanny hated to see her only daughter leave home but knew in her heart of hearts Nathan was the best man for her.

Audie had been gone for five years. He was planning on a visit back to Tennessee by the end of the summer. Fanny counted the days in each month, anxiously waiting the day he was to arrive. He would be here for two weeks, and then he was taking a new assignment in Ethiopia. Even farther away, Fanny thought with dismay.

At least she would be able to savor her short time with him in August. She made plans with Vera to make all his favorite foods. She spoke to his friends at the church, and they planned a party to welcome him home. It became the focal point of her waking hours, waiting until she could see her firstborn son, face to face, once again.

In the meantime, Toby was working hard. He had been employed at the granary two years now. Although they had been forced to find other ways to see one another, Sarah's parents still were unaware of the relationship between the two of them.

Sarah would be seventeen this July. Surely her parents would allow her to see whom she pleased by that time. He had been working steadily; that ought to account for something. All his bad behavior as a wanton youth could surely be set aside with all the progress he had made.

He told Sarah at their last meeting that he wanted to tell her parents about the two of them. She had agreed the time was right. Then calamity struck Toby. His old girlfriend, Lucy, came to him with disturbing news. She was pregnant.

Lucy knew who the father was but was unwilling to say because her paw would force her to marry him. The man was a hard-drinking, disabled man who had fathered the child. Lucy couldn't bear the thought of being the wife of this man the rest of her life. So she told her father that Toby Small was the baby's father.

Toby looked at Lucy incredulously. How could she do such a thing, he demanded of her.

"Toby, I *had* to. Don't you see, I had no choice." Her eyes pleaded with Toby to understand.

"Lucy, I can't marry you! I…there's someone else I love," he said softly.

"Well, I'm sorry for that, Toby. But my paw is going to come looking for you," Lucy said, "and he is going to make you marry me." Lucy looked frail and sad, standing in front of him, her arms crossed against her chest.

"I'll tell him the truth," Toby said. "He's a reasonable man. He'll understand."

Lucy gave a small grunt, "He'll believe me over you,"

"Please, Lucy, don't do this to me or to yourself," Toby begged his former girlfriend. "I would never force you to do something like this."

"Well, you ain't the one gonna have this here baby, now, are ya?" She looked at Toby, with a defiance he knew he could not easily win against.

"I can't marry you," he said firmly, "and I won't."

"We'll see about that," she replied, and turning her back to him, she strode off down the tree-lined back road to her home.

54

Waiting for an Answer

A million or more thoughts coursed through Toby's mind. How was he going to remedy this situation? Lucy was right. Her paw would never believe him over her. Truth to tell, Toby hadn't been with Lucy or any other girl that way since he started keeping company with Sarah, but how could he even begin to prove it? All day at his work, the thoughts plagued him. At home, during supper, he was uncharacteristically quiet. Even his mother's talk of Audie's impending visit could bring no comment from his lips.

"Toby?" Fanny repeated. "I've asked you twice now, what is bothering you? You've barely touched your food."

"I guess...I'm just not that hungry," he answered.

"Well, you need to eat. How will you have strength to work if you don't eat?" Fanny prodded him.

"I have to go somewhere," Toby said, rising from his chair.

"Where?" his mother inquired.

"Just out," he said.

In the twilight, he walked to clear his head. If he had believed that God cared, he might have prayed for an answer. Why would God care? Toby had never taken God seriously before. God would know that. But maybe...he was desperate for help.

He started out slow. "God, I'm in trouble. I don't know what to do. I'm sure you already know all about it, so I won't bother you with the details. Please, can you, just this once, do this for me? Just tell me what to do." He looked up to the heavens as if the answer would somehow appear in the clouds or the setting sun. No answer came to him.

If he waited Lucy's paw out, he would come looking for him. If he went to talk to him prior to that, her paw would just think he was trying to get out of his obligation to his daughter. Unless he could somehow prove that Lucy had been with someone else instead of him. But how?

It all seemed so hopeless. Why had he ever had anything to do with someone like Lucy? She was what some folks defined as poor white trash. Their home was little more than a shack. Her paw made moonshine for money. Her maw was a haggard-looking woman who never smiled and spent most of her time sitting on the front porch, drinking her husband's homemade liquor. Was it any wonder Lucy turned out as she had?

Toby remembered when the home he grew up in was in the same condition as Lucy's. However, when his maw gave her heart to the Lord, everything changed for the better. This gave him a little hope in a merciful God.

In the meantime, Toby would wait. He wanted to see if God was really listening to his prayer. If He was, surely an answer would come. If not, he didn't know where he would be this time next year. He wanted to see Sarah. He just needed to hold her, to have her tell him everything would be all right. Of course, he couldn't tell her about Lucy. She would never understand. Maybe they should go ahead with their plans to tell her parents about the two of them. It's not like anyone else knew about Lucy. If they had her parents' approval, it would go a long way toward cementing things between the two of them. Yes, he told himself, that was the best course of action to take.

Gratified that he had come to this decision, Toby headed back home. When he saw Sarah, they would set a time to speak to her parents. *It really would all work out*, he thought, *after all*.

❖———❖

He met Sarah near the general store. This was their meeting place when Sarah's mother sent her for grocery items once a week.

"When would be a good time to speak to your parents?" he asked her.

"I was thinking about that. Toby, I think we should postpone it." She looked at him with timidity.

"What? Why? I thought you wanted to tell them about us…we agreed…at least, I thought we did."

"I know, but they are so busy and stressed with Papa's banking business slowing down. And then Mama, she's actually been talking about taking a job outside the house to help. That's really been upsetting my father too. It's really not the best time, Toby."

"Will there ever *be* a good time to tell them?" Toby asked in exasperation.

"Yes, of course. Just give it a little time, please, Toby."

He shrugged in resignation, "All right. I guess we have no choice." He looked at her with pain in his eyes. *She was so beautiful*, he thought, *there's nothing I wouldn't do for her. Even it took moving heaven and earth.*

<hr/>

Toby knew the time was short before Mr. Dowdy would come hunting for him with his shotgun. He wasn't going to run from it. He would stand up like a man and tell the truth. At least, that way, he would be holding on to his integrity.

In the meantime, he decided to try to talk sense into Lucy. He went to see her after he finished at the granary. He stood out front of the ramshackle house her family lived in. He called for her, hoping her paw would not come out.

Lucy appeared through a crack in the old wooden door. She saw it was Toby and came out onto the porch.

"I need to talk to you, Lucy," he said firmly.

"Fine by me," she replied, with equal firmness in her voice.

"Can we take a walk or something?" Toby said, not wishing to be overheard.

Lucy shrugged her thin shoulders, saying, "All right."

"Lucy," Toby began, "suppose you loved someone with all heart, with all your might, with everything you have inside of you, would you want to be railroaded into being with someone else?"

"I already do love someone like that," she said, stopping. She looked directly into Toby's eyes, and she continued, "I've always loved you, Toby. From the very beginning, back when we was just kids."

"Lucy...please. If you really love me, you won't do this to me. You won't be happy, no matter what you may think now." His voice was thick with emotion, rife with desperation.

"Like you even care. Don't matter to you what happens to me." Lucy's tears streaked down her face. She truly looked pitiful.

"That's not true, Lucy. I care...I just care in a different sort of way."

"Well, I guess you think I ain't as good as yer pretty li'l blond girl," Lucy retorted. "Yeah, that's right. I knows all about yer li'l girlfriend. Jes 'cause we ain't got the money for a fancy house an' such you don't want to be married to someone like me. Well, you just kin go back an' tell yer li'l girl that it's all over between you and her. I love you, and I'm bound to be yer wife."

Lucy started to walk away, but Toby grabbed her arm.

"Lucy, I've tried to get you to understand," he said through clenched teeth. His grip on Lucy's arm tightened.

"Stop it! Yer hurtin' me!" She attempted to wrest her arm out of his vice-like grip.

Toby pulled her closer, and he placed his hand over her mouth, still holding tightly to her arm.

"Listen to me! I'm *not* going to marry you! Get that through your head! I don't want to hurt you, but you have to understand!" Toby was filled with a rage he didn't know he could feel. He felt as though he could easily snap Lucy's neck in two. He dropped both his hands to his sides and turned away from her. He covered his face with his hands.

"We'll see about that," Lucy said and took off running toward her house.

Fanny had put Toby's name into the prayer circle, saying the Lord knew all about her requests. Now, at home, sitting in her familiar rocker, she stared into the fireplace, watching the flames leap. She wished she knew what was bothering him. God had answered her prayers and brought him back to the right path in life, only to have him distraught and distracted. She prayed that God would help him with whatever it was he was facing. Please help him, Lord Jesus, she prayed.

55

Best of Plans

That day at the granary was unbearably long. Toby felt like his watch had stopped; time was moving so slowly. He was very anxious to talk to Sarah. He had formed a plan to counter Lucy's accusations.

Lucy wanted to marry him, but she wouldn't be able to even if her paw held him at gunpoint—not if he was already married. It seemed like the perfect solution to him. He just had to get Sarah on board. Somehow, he had to convince her that an elopement would be the best thing all around.

Sarah's parents wouldn't be able to object once they were married, and Lucy wouldn't be able to extort him with her lie. It all depended on convincing Sarah.

Finally, the dismissal bell sounded for Toby's shift. He left before anyone could say anything to him. He and Sarah were supposed to meet in back of the Baptist church at 4:00 p.m. If he went now, he'd be waiting for a half hour, but that was fine with him. There was no need to go home first and have to contend with his mother's questions about where he was going. This was the better way.

Having reached the back of the churchyard, Toby was too nervous to sit. He paced back and forth, thinking of what words he would use to persuade Sarah to elope with him. His watch, once again, seemed to move unutterably slow. When he saw Sarah coming down the footpath through the woods, he ran to meet her.

When they met one another, Toby enveloped Sarah in his arms and buried his face in her shoulder. The smell of her hair was fragrant like honeysuckle. It only reminded him of how much he loved her.

"Toby!" she exclaimed. "I swear you're going to break my ribs!" she laughed lightly and smiled at him.

Her smile faded when she realized how serious the expression on his face was.

"What's wrong?" she questioned him.

"Nothings wrong," he began hesitantly. "I just have something real important to talk to you about, is all."

"All right. What is it?"

"You have to promise me something first," Toby said this, looking deep into her violet eyes.

"What?" Sarah was concerned now to the point of fear.

"Promise me..." he started, slowly but deliberately, "promise me that you won't say 'no' right away. Promise you'll think about it really well before you make a decision." He held her at arms' length, still trying to penetrate her eyes with his own. Sarah had never seen Toby be so earnest regarding anything.

"All right then," she said, "I promise."

"I want to elope with you." He put one finger over her lips as he saw her begin to protest.

"Please, hear me out." he continued. "If we do that, your parents won't be able to undo it. They will have to accept it, and you know they will. It will save us both a lot of heartache."

"Oh, Toby, I don't know," she shook her head, contemplating the whole idea.

"You want to marry me, right?" he asked her, once again, eyes pleading with her.

"Of course, I do…" she admitted, "but, it's just a lot to think about…"

"I know, but really, I believe it would be the best thing for us to do."

Sarah looked at Toby. She couldn't understand why he seemed so agitated and urgent. It scared her a little. She hoped he was not in any kind of trouble. Although she feared hearing his answer, she forced herself to say, "Toby, why is this so important all of a sudden? You're not in any trouble, are you?" She searched his face for a clue to what was the matter.

"No, of course not," he said, but now, he averted his gaze from hers. "I just don't want to wait any longer. I love you, and I want us to be together."

"When do you need an answer?" she asked him finally.

"By this time tomorrow," he said.

❖────────❖

The following day, time crept for Toby. He was so nervous his hands visibly shook. He found he kept having to shake his hands out, trying to get it under control. He took deep breaths, hoping his supervisor wasn't aware of anything amiss.

Once again, Toby went to his and Sarah's meeting place. This time, she was there ahead of him. He hoped that was a good sign. When he was close enough to hear her reply, he said, "Well?" expectantly.

"Yes, I'll go with you," and she held out her arms to him, smiling. Toby felt a flood of relief sweep over him. *Thank you, Jesus*, he thought to himself, *things were going to work out after all!* He was so relieved, he laughed out loud.

Sarah started laughing also, and together, they fell to the ground, embracing, and laughing until they could laugh no more.

"Be ready tomorrow morning," he instructed her, serious once again. "I'll come by your house at 5:00 a.m., before your folks wake up. Can you be ready by then?"

"Yes," she agreed, "I'll be ready."

56

Overheard

Lucy Dowdy often fled her home when her father flew into one of his drunken rages. This left only her mother and younger brother for him to turn his anger against. Times such as these, Lucy would escape into the woods surrounding the house she had been born in and lived in since that.

She had become an expert at navigating her way through tree limbs, dense shrubbery, and the like over the years. She loved the woods. There, she found peace in the surrounding nature, solace in the sounds of leaving murmuring in the summer breeze and the sound her feet made when they pressed down on ancient vines.

Paw had come in drunk again. He drank from sun up to sun down, so it was not unusual. He drank while tending his still just beyond the house, carefully camouflaged by the woods. By the time he had made a batch of whiskey, he had already ingested about as much. Lucy had a love-hate relationship with her paw. He was her paw, so she was required by blood to love him. And she hated him because he was a hateful, drunken abuser.

Today, she left before he even noticed she was gone. Walking carefully, she made her way through the thickest part of the woods. Sometimes, she found a tree with low-hanging branches. She used these to climb onto the tree, finding a perch from which she could look out at the whole world that was Porter's Bend. It was really amazing what you could see from up there.

She did not feel like tree climbing today though. She pushed her flyaway blond hair behind her ears to keep it from falling into her eyes. She was coming to the opposite edge of woods from the house. She heard voices. She stopped, listened. A man and a woman's voices, too far to distinguish what was being said. She crept, Indian-like, closer to the clearing, making sure her feet made no noise.

She peered through the trees, noting the Baptist church to the left. She saw before hearing them. It was Toby and that girl, the girl he claimed to be in love with. Lucy hated her without knowing her. She strained her ears to hear the conversation.

So they're running away. *He thinks that will get him out of marrying me*, she thought. *Hmph.* Lucy touched her abdomen where the fetus grew within her. Her eyes filled with tears. It seemed she had never had anyone who really loved her. Not her paw, nor her maw. Not even the many boys and men she had given herself to. They had only pretended to care about her. It would not be that way for her baby. No, it would not. Not even if she had to lie, steal, beg, no matter what. She would make sure this baby had love.

Lucy heard Toby set the time they were leaving. She stood still, motionless. She began to consider all the possibilities.

57

Audie Comes Home

The train station was only moderately busy the day Audie arrived in Kingston. A few people stood at the ticket desk buying their way out of the city. Several sat on benches waiting on layovers or for the next outgoing train. Fanny and Jane went to the gate to await the train Audie was to come in on.

Jane and Nathan had made arrangements to come to Tennessee as soon as the word came to them about Audie's visit. Nathan had stayed behind with their two children at Fanny's house. Toby was God knows where, Fanny was thinking.

Both women were waiting anxiously for son and brother to appear from the many passengers that exited the train. It seemed to Fanny that the line of people would never end, when she saw him. He seemed taller than he had when she last saw him. Of course he would be, she chided herself.

Audie saw his mother and Jane right off and walked up and hugged them both, one arm encircling each one.

"Momma…Sissy…I can't believe I'm really here!" he exulted.

"Oh, honey, you look…so grown up!" Fanny cried, tears coming, though she tried mightily to stem the flow.

"I am grown up, Momma. Janie, you're a married woman and a mother now!" He held her at arm's length as if to inspect her. Jane smiled, so happy to see her brother again.

"Audie, you've grown a foot!" she said, hugging him again.

"So where is that little brother of mine?" Audie asked, hoping "jail" would not be the answer.

"I…he probably had to work late. You know, he does sometimes." Fanny hoped her expression was not giving away her fears as to Toby's whereabouts.

"He's really been doing well, up to this point…," Fanny's voice trailed off. Then, to change the subject, she said, "Vera is planning a welcome home dinner for you, Audie. Isn't that wonderful of her to do?"

"Great! Bring on the fried chicken! Do you know what I've had to eat the past five years?" Audie laughed and said, "I'm not complaining, though. I thank the good Lord just to have had something to eat!"

They all laughed. Audie said he was proud to be escorting such beautiful women through the city. Jane replied with, "And we ladies are with the handsomest man!" The three of them were giddy with the feeling only being with one's family can bring.

In honor of the occasion, Fanny even paid the fare for a taxi cab to take them all to Vera's house. Audie protested, but she insisted. "Money well spent," she said firmly. Jane said she couldn't wait for Audie to see his niece and nephew, not to mention his brother-in-law.

If only Toby had been with them, everything would have been perfect, Fanny thought. But even that would not spoil this time for her. She wouldn't allow it. Everything was very near perfect.

58

Tragedy

Upon the family's arrival, Nathan introduced his son and daughter to their uncle. Nathan Jr. and Dorthea were shy with Audie at first but soon warmed up to his charm. He willingly played horsy, galloping on all fours while both children laughed. He told them stories of his adventures in El Salvador. They listened, along with the adults, wide-eyed with interest.

Dorthea made the announcement that she too wanted to be a missionary one day. Jane told her daughter that it was a noble calling but much hard work. Dorthea told her mother that would be no problem. She would just take along her big brother, Nate, to help her. The adults smiled indulgently at the childish prattle.

Fanny kept looking at the clock on Vera's wall. She would have thought Toby would surely have shown up by this time. After the supper was eaten and compliments given out appropriately to their cook, Fanny and Jane began the clearing of dishes. It was around this time that Toby walked through the front door.

"Toby!" Audie was up and embracing his younger brother before Toby even had a chance to react to it.

"Toby, where have you been?" Fanny questioned him in a tone that spoke of her disappointment in him for being so late.

"I'm sorry, Maw," Toby replied. "I had some important business to take care of," he continued.

"You sure look great, Audie," he said, looking at his brother.

"What about me?" Jane stood, hands on hips, a smile creeping onto her face, as she teased Toby.

"You look wonderful of course, Jane. And real grown up too," he said, and turning to Nathan, he shook his hand.

When the small talk all around was finished, a silence filled the room.

"Well, Jane, let's get these dishes into the kitchen," Fanny said, breaking the awkward pause in conversation.

The women gathered the dishes while the men went into the front parlor. Toby fell slightly behind Audie and whispered to Nathan, "I have to tell you something."

Nathan looked at Toby, wondering what mischief he had gotten into now.

When all of them were seated, Toby took a deep breath and said, "I'm leaving in the morning,"

"Where to?" Audie asked.

"I'm leaving with Sarah Brewster…we're eloping." Toby, usually direct in speech, faltered now.

"Does Momma know about this?" Audie asked him.

"No, not yet. I was kind of hoping…one of you two could tell her for me…please?" Toby looked so solemn, so scared.

"You should really be the one to do that, Toby," Nathan remarked. Nathan was someone who always followed the rules in such situations.

"No, I can't…she'll only fuss and try to talk me out of it…and there's just no other way," Toby's tone was firm.

"Why do you say it that way?" Audie wanted to know. "She's not…you know…?"

"No, of course not. It's not about that. You have to take my word for it." Toby's eyes met those of his brother. Audie could see his brother was not lying.

"When are you leaving tomorrow? Can we see you off, at least?" Audie inquired.

"I told Sarah to be ready at 5:00 a.m. outside her house. From there, we'll go to the train station. I figure Jonestown would be the best place to go."

Audie and Nathan fell silent, neither of them sure what to say now.

They may have been that way for a couple of minutes or so. The quiet in the room was broken by a loud pounding on Vera's front door. Audie rose to see who was there. Generally speaking, folks didn't call socially at this time of evening unless it was urgent. The pounding had that urgency behind it.

Upon opening the front door, Audie saw a weathered, haggard older man saunter into Vera's foyer. He wore ragged overalls over a tattered flannel shirt. A rifle was in his hands, and he seemed to be ready to use it.

"Where is he?" the man demanded.

By this time, the women had come out of the kitchen and stood, in the background, listening.

"Toby Small, that's who," the old man stated. "My girl's with child, and he's the father of it," he declared loudly.

Fanny had recognized the visitor as Hank Dowdy, father of Lucy Dowdy. Fanny didn't know the family well, but she was well acquainted with the reputation of the daughter. It was also widely talked of that Mr. Dowdy was a bootlegger. Fanny had long been afraid of this very scenario happening, and now it had.

Toby strode into the foyer, facing Hank Dowdy.

"Mr. Dowdy," Toby's voice shook as he told him, "I know what Lucy says, but you got to believe me...I am *not* the father of that baby."

"She's says dif'rent." He held the rifle, aiming it right at Toby's chest.

"I know...but, it's just not true." Toby stood and looked directly at Hank Dowdy.

"Well, it's like this," the old man stated, "you marry my Lucy, or yer mama gonna be buryin'ya."

"No," Toby said this quietly.

Audie tried to say something to diffuse the tense situation.

"This is not the way to handle this, sir," directing his comment to Hank.

"It's *my* way," he replied dully. Audie could smell the whiskey, and the eyes of Hank Dowdy were glazed over drunkenly.

Audie placed his hand on the rifle barrel, trying to lower the muzzle. Hank jerked back suddenly, and an explosive noise rocked the house. It reverberated throughout the walls, floor, and ceiling. The women were screaming and crying at the same time.

And, there, on the tiled floor of Vera Reynolds's foyer lay Audie, eyes open, a look of surprise etched on his face.

Fanny rushed to him. Using a dish towel, she helplessly attempted to stem the blood flowing from his chest wound. She kept screaming his name over and over. Audie could not answer her. The rifle shell had penetrated his heart muscle, bringing death immediately.

Everyone was spellbound for what seemed like hours. Fanny's cries dwindled to a jagged, "No, no." Nathan regained his senses first, heading out the back door, figuring to find law enforcement across the bridge.

Hank Dowdy disappeared into the night. Vera got a blanket and covered up Audie's body. Jane knelt beside her mother, one arm surrounding her shoulders.

Toby stood there. The whole scene seemed unreal, like a bad dream that had no end. He didn't know what he should do or say, so he just stood there. That's where he was when Nathan returned with the Kingston police.

The officer told all of them the coroner was notified and would be sending a wagon for Audie's body. Toby had stood there in the foyer, looking down at his mother and his sister kneeling at the side of his brother's body. He felt numb and as though he couldn't move. Vera came up to him and led him away, into the other room. She got him into a chair and went to get Fanny and Jane. She didn't want them to see the coroner take Audie away.

59

Joy in the Morning

Vera made sure Fanny, Toby, and Jane were not where they could see the coroner's people take Audie away to the city morgue. Even though she was not related to Audie by blood, her heart still broke to see them place his body on a gurney, cover it with a sheet, and take him out of her house forever. How much more so for his real family, she thought to herself.

Fanny was numb. She felt no emotions, which surprised her. She wondered if she would ever feel anything, ever again. It didn't seem possible that she could. She was so dead inside right now; how could she ever feel emotion again? Indeed, if not for the memories of having joy, despair, anger, happiness, and a myriad of emotions, she would not have known their existence at all. Surely this was a blessing from God. It was His way of allowing her to cope with facts too horrible to contemplate.

Jane was equally non-emotional. She had traveled all these miles between Tennessee and Alabama, only to experience this tragedy. If she had not come, would it still have ended up this way? She found it strange that her mind went in this direction when she should be thinking of Audie. But, what to think of him? He was gone from this life. No more teasing from a big brother, no encouraging words, not even a letter that travels hundreds of miles to reach the receiver. Her mind could not conceive of it.

Toby was seized with a very real emotion: anger. Anger at Hank Dowdy for taking his only brother's life, and Lucy Dowdy for having set this chain of events in motion. He sat, hands clenched into fists, his mind ablaze with thoughts of retaliation. They were all a bunch of dumb hillbillies, he thought with disgust, which was almost as livid as the rage seething just below the surface. He should have killed Lucy when he had the chance. When she told him the bald-faced lie she was telling her father about the pregnancy he himself had nothing to do with. How dare she? Little tramp of a woman. And that drunken whiskey-chugging madman she called a father.

"Ahhh!" He inadvertently let a scream escape him. He pounded the arms of the chair he sat in over and over again. Vera rushed into the room. She saw Fanny and Jane, sitting together on the settee, looking at Toby as if he were an alien. Toby sat, looking like a truly tortured soul, pounding the chair. W hen he looked up at Vera, remorse flooded his face, and he crumpled, like a scarecrow taken from its perch, into himself. He cried loud, gut-wrenching cries that came from some where deep inside of him. Vera went to him and cradled his massive shoulders into her arms. She held him until the cries ceased.

✦────✦

The funeral was over now. Hundreds flooded the Baptist Church in Porter's Bend. There were more people there for Audie Small's funeral than any other event ever held there. Nathan, Jane, and their children were back in Alabama. Fanny was left alone; her grief was shared with church folks. Some of those had lost sons or daughters and knew time alone could ease the pain.

Hank Dowdy was arrested and was being held in the Kingston city jail awaiting arraignment. There would be an indictment then a trial. This was a scandal in the small community of Porter's Bend where such things were rare. The revenue people came and dismantled the still Hank had kept hidden in the woods. Now, his family was forced to find other ways to produce an income, namely, the welfare system in the state of Tennessee. This was, ultimately, good for Lucy. The state would pay for doctor's visits and any other prenatal care she required.

Toby was forced by the situation to tell Sarah the whole sordid story—all the way from Lucy's lie to his brother's death. News of Audie's untimely death reached all areas, including those beyond Porter's Bend and even beyond Kingston. There was no reason to hide Toby's and Sarah's relationship from her parents any longer. Together, they admitted the secrecy of their meetings over the past two years. Although troubled that Sarah hadn't approached them sooner, they accepted the reasons the couple gave them. Sarah's mother, especially, realized how difficult she must have made things for her daughter. She grieved that she hadn't made her feel she could have confided in her. She promised her she would never again repeat that mistake.

Families who love one another with the love of the Lord can always find the strength to work through challenging times. Toby and Sarah wanted the Brewsters to see how much they loved one another and set a wedding date for the following year.

Toby gave his whole heart to God, and both Sarah and he began to attend church. He realized how God had been faithful to protect and love him throughout every situation. He was especially grateful for the love of his wife-to-be.

The Small family, Fanny and her children, had been through joyous and tragic events. Still, they continued, each on their own path. God had used good and bad times to bring out the best part of each of them that sought to know Him. It truly was a work in progress. Fanny had gone from a child, saved and knowledgeable in God's ways, to a woman who lost her way in life and, finally, to find Him again.

Audie had been, from the beginning, one who loved God and wanted to serve him with every fiber within himself. If it is true that the good die young, it was exceptionally true for Audie.

Jane also found God early in life, and He had guided her every decision. He had always made her feel safe and protected, just as her older brother had. She was thankful she had a life away from the painful memories of life with Audie in it. It was not because he hadn't loved her that made those memories painful, but rather, because he had. Ultimately, she accepted God's perfect will, though she didn't understand it.

Toby found a woman's love and journeyed on to find the greatest love of all—the love of God. He vowed never to take Sarah or his God for granted.

As Fanny reflected on the life she had lived, she marveled at the goodness of her God—His forgiving nature always abounding toward us. She had lost Audie, her beloved son. Yet she realized she hadn't really lost him, but that he was rejoicing in glory and she would see him again one day. Jesus gave her reassurance, blessed reassurance. Audie had not died in vain but in protecting his loved ones.

Each person had experienced God in different ways. It was a journey each had to walk for himself. Fanny was so glad all her children knew Jesus as their savoir. She could see His hand in her life, even when she rejected Him. Her soul rejoiced in reading Psalm 30:5, "Weeping may endure for the night, but Joy cometh in the morning." She lifted her hands in worship, praising her God. She knew His word was true! He had allowed the weeping but had brought her to Joy unspeakable! Praise Him!

CPSIA information can be obtained
at www.ICGtesting.com
Printed in the USA
FSOW04n1707061016
25767FS